SIRENS

BIRTH OF VENGEANCE

ARIES KING

Copyright © 2023 Aries King.

All rights reserved. No part of this book may be reproduced, stored, or transmitted by any means—whether auditory, graphic, mechanical, or electronic—without written permission of both publisher and author, except in the case of brief excerpts used in critical articles and reviews. Unauthorized reproduction of any part of this work is illegal and is punishable by law.

ISBN: 979-8-89031-399-7 (sc)
ISBN: 979-8-89031-400-0 (hc)
ISBN: 979-8-89031-401-7 (e)

Because of the dynamic nature of the Internet, any web addresses or links contained in this book may have changed since publication and may no longer be valid. The views expressed in this work are solely those of the author and do not necessarily reflect the views of the publisher, and the publisher hereby disclaims any responsibility for them.

One Galleria Blvd., Suite 1900, Metairie, LA 70001
1-888-421-2397

CONTENTS

Acknowledgments v

Chapter 1   Invisible Scars 1

Chapter 2   Just Getting By 10

Chapter 3   Battle Lines..16

Chapter 4   Familiar Ghosts 26

Chapter 5   Curiosity Kills 35

Chapter 6   Middle Men 41

Chapter 7   City Under Siege...50

Chapter 8   Uncomfortable Truths 61

Chapter 9   XXX-Posed..67

Chapter 10 Friend or Foe 75

Chapter 11 Alpha Female...82

Chapter 12 Aftermath 91

Chapter 13 Direct Hit..97

Chapter 14 Crossing the Line 103

Chapter 15 Girl Fight...110

Chapter 16 Student vs. Teacher 119

Chapter 17 Odd Alliances..124

Chapter 18 Unusual Suspects...132

Chapter 19 No Truce 139

Chapter 20 Final Resolution 147

Chapter 21 Sisters 157

ACKNOWLEDGMENTS

This being the first of many flights of imagination, I want to thank those without whom none of this would be possible.

First, I must give all Praise, Honor, and Glory to Christ who protects, guides, strengthens, and inspires me daily. You have made me the man I am and have blessed me with all that I have. I'm so unapologetically grateful for all that You are in my life. I am forever indebted and humbled by your Majesty, Power, and Mercy. Amen.

To my Mother, SGA: You have always been my biggest fan and my greatest supporter. You allowed me to reach for stars I could only imagine and assured me they were there for me to grab onto if I only work hard and believe. You taught me better than anyone else could have, how to be a good man. I consider you my ultimate blessing because without your guidance and encouragement I might never have found my way. Yours is the example of strength, resilience, determination, and integrity that I draw from in my walk. I thank and Love you, Momma.

To my Brother, DEM: You are the only man who's ever been constant in my life. In you, I see all the heart and kindness I needed to give me hope to press on. You are my hero and I Love you more than I can ever truly express. God couldn't have blessed me with a better Big Brother. I will always cherish our bond. Love you, Dada.

FWBC: I would like to thank my extended family of Faith at Friendship-West-Baptist-Church in Dallas TX especially my Pastor Dr. Frederick D. Haynes III. You have all been so welcoming encouraging and supportive. From the Ministers to the staff, OMG, and the Members I have never before felt such a strong sense of belonging. To my Pastor, my mentor, and my friend Dr. Haynes, you inspire me to fight for those who can't fight for themselves as you fight so tirelessly for us all. I thank you.

To the Brothers of Kappa Alpha Psi Fraternity Inc. I love all you guys and appreciate the bond we share in Phi Nu Pi. Your support and belief in my talent means the world to me and I can't thank you brothers enough for your help in bringing these dreams of mine to fruition. Nupe Nupe Yo!!!

CHAPTER 1

INVISIBLE SCARS

DISCLAIMER —Let me just start by saying, this is not some sort of fake O.J. Simpson professionally written diary, nor is it an admission of any guilt. Truthfully, in thinking about the circumstances of all this craziness; I feel totally vindicated—No shame. Nope, I've made peace with exactly who I am and what I've done—so this is just me telling you how it all happened.

You may be asking, 'Who the hell hand writes their memoirs?' Well, this was never a story I intended to tell. As a matter of fact, if it hadn't been for all the lies being spread in the blogosphere, my lips would still be sealed.

Anywayz, my name is Jeadda. I'm a twenty-five-year-old former Exotic Dancer and this is the story of how I became a Siren. If you're reading this, you've probably already been bombarded with all of the propaganda surrounding my comrades and me. The talking heads call us vigilantes and assassins—anything to discredit our purpose and nullify our contribution to the safety of the citizens of San Francisco. They criticize our methods while completely ignoring the results. I guess vilifying us was the only way the S.F.P.D. could cover up their incompetent handling of the matter.

For me, the whole thing began on a brutally cold winter's night, in the basement dressing room of Club Eye Candy. If you've never been, it's as sleazy as you might imagine, but at least the drinks are pretty good and we've got some of the baddest bitches this side of Rancho Coochee-racha.

My boss—'Sir Mont'e,' is a perfect example of the type of people who frequent the joint. This guy's been hustling since he strolled out of the womb. I thought his kind died out with the Disco Era, but no. SuperFly is alive and well in this flamboyant soul brother with P-Funk vibes, channeled into everything from his eccentric fashion taste to the club's "Boogie Nights" decor.

Our main floor, with its 'charming' purple velvet and silver mylar accents, is a splendid example of 'Renaissance Pimp.' Seriously, the place looks like, somebody murdered a grade school Valentine's Day card in there. But if you're looking for the perfect booze-fueled Bachelor Party venue or a place where you can convince yourself you're God's gift to women; Eye Candy is tailor-made for you.

On, to the 'Dressing-room', painted sterile grey like an afterthought, half-Broadway chorus-line dressing room; half-High School gym locker room. It houses all the traditional relics of the burlesque industry. From the heavy-duty practice stripper pole to the cheesy vanity stations, overflowing with glitters and glosses, false eyelashes, clip-on extensions, and body sprays.

There's a closet full of character props for girls whose lack of talent forces them to rely on such cliché gimmicks. Our shower room doubles as a carpet-muncher paradise for 'ladies who can't control their hormones long enough for their shifts to end.

I sit on the bench situated next to my locker, trying not to notice **_her_** looking at me again—in that strange way she has. You know, the same glassy-eyed stare guys give you before they attack your face with their tongues—I can't help it. She always weirds me out 'cuz it feels like she's gonna try and kiss me... or worse.

Don't get me wrong, Deseree is gorgeous, and if I ran THAT WAY, I could certainly do a lot worse. But I can't even summon up enough curiosity to see if going that route would make my pussy cat purr. Still—to each her own.

Her voice, husky and laced with pre-sex languor, breaks into my thoughts. "Oooow Girl!—and then what happened?" she breathes. She's chewing that wad of strawberry-flavored gum. I can smell it's too-sweet scent, hanging thick in the air. She straddles the plank-wood slab in front of me, her sinewy body clothed in a metallic blue bikini.

Deseree Woods is her name; can you believe it... WOOD? Anyway, her stage name is Cherokee, ever since the night she trotted in claiming to be half Indian. Now, she wears her hair in twin braided ponytails. I'm just waiting for the eagle feathers and war paint to appear.

I can't say she's totally Lesbi-gay or whatever. It's not like she's ever tried anything around me. There's just that aforementioned tingle I get whenever she stares at me. Still, as friends go, she's pretty thorough.

I force my mind to travel back, deep into the past. To the night that gunned down my youth with a single bullet and hurtled me along a twisted path dead-ending me here.

Suddenly, I'm a terrified child again, standing in the living room, while huge men stride passed me—laying waste to everything that made our house a home. As the tears stream from my eyes, I glance over to my mother's lifeless body, tossed in the corner like an old rug. I still remember her smooth, Afro-Peruvian skin that gleamed like a third-place medal.

My father, a Cajun-Creole businessman and Realtor by trade, always carried himself proud and strong. But you'd never know that, by the way they had him slumped on his knees in the middle of the floor—beaten into last Tuesday.

I wanted to run to him; throw myself over him and end the senseless nightmare, but I was frozen in terror. The men ignored me mostly and continued their savage work. One of them turned his head in my direction. He was an Ogre: The man they called Blakk. My fear seemed to feed him. Before I knew it, he was crouched beside me, resting his massive forearm around my shoulders. Pulling me uncomfortably close to his shaggy face:

"Yuh love yuh fadda?" he growled in a gravely Caribbean accent—thanks to a lifetime, hand-rolled cigarette habit. The aroma of Brut cologne and cheap booze assaulted my nostrils.

Who were these men? How did they know my Pappa? What had he done to deserve this?

Another huge Island man, a clear-cut psycho they called REESE. He held a gun to my father's head, crowing, "Less jus kill dem 'n get di 'el out from ir!" His face twitched, a manic defect of the conflicting personalities living within him.

"Since when do you make decisions, Reese... I say what we do!" a cold, steel-tempered voice rumbled. And there he was—the Devil himself. In all the confusion, I hadn't noticed him sitting in Pappa's reading chair. A titanic monolith of a man, cloaked in shadow and surrounded by a billowy cloud of smoke. To them he was 'Boss'; to me, he was simply, Death—the Grim Reaper incarnate.

I struggled to find the courage, "Y-yes," I whispered.

Blakk pulled me closer to his ear. "Whas dat yuh say, Baby gyal?" he prodded. "Mi canna ir yuh."

"Yes... I love him," I repeated in a cracked voice.

Pappa lifted his head—his face, drenched with his own blood. His eyes strained to find me and when they finally caught me, he managed a pained smile. "Don't be afraid, baby. Daddy loves you."

Blakk's cruel grin widened as he watched my father. It made me hate him all the more. I wanted to save Pappa, but I was too small. I wanted to fight back, but I was too weak; too scared.

"Boss?" he confirmed.

Blakk is then given a detached nod from the shadow—not a word, just that, a fucking nod... My Pappa had raised himself up from the slums of Santo Domingo D.R. and migrated to America a wealthy businessman, in a time when that sort of fantastical shit wasn't happening—he deserved more than that.

Without hesitation, Blakk threw open his jacket and retrieved a massive cannon of a pistol. Grabbing my hand, he forced my finger over the trigger, then raised my arm, and aimed the gun at Pappa. I fought with every bit of strength I could muster but I was as useless as I feared. All I could do was stare down the length of his burly arm, which suddenly seemed to have a gun muzzle grafted onto the end of it.

"It's okay baby," my father repeated.

I clenched my eyes tight and petitioned this God character, Pappa always spoke to. I begged Him to intervene—but nothing. Blakk never stopped smiling the entire time—It was all a sick joke to him.

"Please... no please," I begged.

—and then suddenly, BOWOOMB!!!

The explosion was deafening and reverberated throughout my body like an earthquake jolt, into my very soul. The recoil jammed the bones in my arm and I caught the mist of gunpowder. I opened my eyes, just in time to see Pappa's body collapse to the floor—as did my heart.

All at once, fear and pain are replaced by the sensation of falling—like the ground dropped out from beneath me. *"He made me kill him."* The words themselves became a haunting refrain I sung inside my skull for the better part of my young life.

That night I became born again, blessed with the Spirit of Vengeance.

I emerge from my flashback and realize I've squeezed the palms of my hands bloodless. Deseree's mouth gapes wider than an open mailbox.

Thankfully, our awkward silence is broken by the very familiar, very loud echo of seven-inch stilettoes tapping their way down the dressing room stairs like a blind man's cane.

"Is you bitches deaf or just dumb?" a voice shrilly demands. Enter, Debra Knox aka 'Cheeks'—veteran stripper, long passed her expiration date, but still hanging on the pole. Cheeks is tall, loud, and abrasive—a social opportunist, about as ghetto-fab as they come. Her face only reads two emotions: Drunk or High. She's been an Eye Candy fixture longer than anyone can remember, sloppily twerking her way through several managers and name changes.

She's also sort of an industry legacy—her mother stripped in the 70's and her father was a pathetic wanna-be stickup kid; until he died during a liquor store robbery when she was just twelve.

People say that's when Cheeks started showing up at the club with her mom. Yeah, I know—It probably wasn't the best place for a 'Bring Your Kid to Work Day.'

"What the hell is you hoes doing down here anyways? Don't yawl know them Dudes is up there tricking?" she trumpets.

Deseree rolls her eyes in my direction—she can't stand the sight of the old-school Alley Cat—her words not mine. I think she reminds Desi of the all-too-harsh VIP room reality she's headed for if things don't take off. Me, I don't mind Cheeks so much. I think of her more as a cautionary tale than a rival.

Cheeks rummages through her locker, a shrine to her career's worth of brief celebrity encounters. Tasteless photos of her with everyone from Rappers to Athletes to known Pimps.

"I'm about to bleed these negros dry!" she proclaims.

"Cheeks, do you mind? This is kind of a private conversation," Deseree warns.

Cheeks has no reference for 'private.' She retrieves a box of condoms and stuffs some in her bra before slamming the door shut. "Whatever. More money for me then!" she diverts, clip-clopping back upstairs, just slow enough to make Deseree steam.

She screws her face and cuts her eyes toward me, "You see what I'm saying," she huffs.

All I can offer is a consoling shrug.

Deseree's face softens. She cups my hand in hers and again, I feel like I'm in the Lion's den. I'm surprised when her expression reveals genuine concern. "So, do you remember what he looked like? You could go to the cops… get them to do one of those drawings."

What an odd question. Of course, I remember… I've been doing my damnedest over the years to forget Blakk's smug, Cheshire cat's grin and evil eyes—but cops? HELL NO! I had already borne witness to just how the 'JUST US' system works. Shitty ass Feds said they were there to help and then did their best to link my father to organized crime and take everything we had.

I used to hear people rage all the time about how 'You can't trust them Suits,' but I just figured they must have done something to deserve what happened to them. But no, those racist pigs showed my little ass the truth of it all—but good.

Now I say, "Fuck the police! Those bastards are more corrupt than the criminals!"

"So… whatever happened to what's her name? Her Daddy got killed too, right?" Deseree's face radiates an ulterior motive.

She means Candace, the only living person on this planet that means anything to me. My sister—my Can-daNce. Candace has been my best friend since Elementary-school. She dances at Alvin Ailey American Dance Theater, now—imagine that? One of the most difficult companies to get into and she made it. Not to mention she looks like an Earth angel or something. But growing up she was just my skinny little tag-along.

"Her name's Candace. She lives in New York, but her family still owns a house out here," I answer.

"The two of you... like, still talk or what?" she digs.

Damn, Lois Lane? Why do you give a shit anyway? "Yeah, we talk. Although, it's mostly been by e-mail, lately. Some best friend I am, huh?" I blurt it out before I can catch myself...

Deseree grins flirtatiously and I immediately realize my mistake. "Best friend? The way you talk about her, I thought she was an old boo of yours."

Shit! I've done it now—opened Pandora's Lesbi-box. My next words may mean the difference between the continuation of our relatively distant association or complete defamation of Deseree's lifestyle—and being that she is the closest thing I have to a confidant in this place, I dare not muddy the waters.

"Girl, please, you know I don't run that way! It's strictly Dickly for me," I joke—hoping to extinguish the growing tension in the already Musky Dungeon.

Deseree gives me an icy nod. "What-ev. Does she know what you do?"

"She knows I dance, but I didn't exactly tell her I'm a private dancer."

Deseree howls with laughter. "Bitch, you a Booty-shaker at best! Just because you show your privates, don't make you no Private Dancer!" We laugh hysterically—me, from relief more than anything.

Suddenly, an overhead intercom squawk breaks up the party. Sir Monte's voice emerges in the static: "Starr to stage 1... Starr, you're up on stage 1!"

"That's you, Private Dancer," Deseree jests.

She gets up to go and I make a quick sweep of my locker. Staring into the full-length mirror with my mother's photo taped to it, I remember. First, that there is no such thing as 'Comfort Fit' thongs, and second, how much a part of me she still is. My shape mimics hers exactly—such that we could have been twins in another life. I wonder what she'd think to see me now. Or, for that matter, what my father would say about my chosen profession. His life plan for me most likely included college, a buttoned-down Conservi-geek husband, and some stuffy office job.

Another announcement over the intercom and I quickly dismiss those thoughts. Time for my customary mental checklist—sequined bikini top adjusted, tits—hoppin'. A shake of my ass confirms, ass—rockin'. A puckered air kiss directed at my mirrored reflection, lips—poppin'.

Only one thing left—a Stripper's affirmation of sorts. Meditation on a simple concept: *"You are in control."* I grab my things, close my locker, and make my way up the stairs to begin my night. *"Rock the Room, Baby-girl..."*

CHAPTER 2

JUST GETTING BY

Standing on stage for the first set of the night is gut-churning every time, no matter how much I've done it. All I can think of is, 'I shouldn't have stopped drinking.' Breathing helps, but it isn't until I feel the music that I'm safe. My audience disappears and I escape into my own world, where the bass pulses through me like my own heartbeat.

Right on cue, the track begins to play—my theme song. Velvet curtains part, and for a moment I can feel their eyes roaming over my body, warming me with their desire like heat lamps. These sex-deprived flesh addicts could start a forest fire.

They lick their lips in anticipation. But who can blame them—my creamy butter toffee skin—luscious wavy hair that cascades down my back like a waterfall—my legs, the product of a fifteen-year obsession with dance. Hell, I could fall in love with myself!

Two micro swatches of cherry red fabric are the only thing protecting 'Victoria's Secrets.' My thong hugs my devilishly round ass and while, in any other place, it might be considered criminal—here, I am a star. Make that, 'Starr.' That name was bestowed upon me, a nervous young girl during her first night on stage, by Deseree. I really should thank her for that someday—but not in the way she wants me to.

At last—the B-line hits! I sway to the beat, grunting and groaning—a super train steam engine warming up. A quick peek over my shoulder verifies my crowd of anxious fanatics is hypnotized by the motion of my hips. Their eyes widen as my velvety Cinna-buns flex with each energetic beat and my worshipers shower me with fresh, crisp donations. 'Oh yeah, I got these Mother Fuckers.'

I strut toward the front of the stage and bend over, wiggling my impressive backside for the fiends, before working my way to the floor for my kitten crawl down a path of big-faced bills. I come back from the music long enough to let my eyes survey them, looking for potential Phillip Drummonds—that's what we girls call them dudes who'd like nothing more than to move you up to their Pent-House for some DIFFERENT STROKES. They never arrive with fewer than six stacks and most times, they don't need to be coerced to give.

A well-dressed Grey-Fox of a Zaddy flicks dollars on stage as I approach. He's not half bad looking either, I think to myself. But, as with all things that seem too good to be true, there must be a flaw. It never fails, there is always some sort of intangible defect with the men I meet here. I guess if there wasn't; I wouldn't meet them here at all. Either way, my keen eye can normally spot deal-breakers a mile away. Hah! That's an unusually healthy attitude for a gal in my profession, don't you think?

"Girl, I want you so bad," Mr. Drummond implores.

Yeah, I'll just bet you do, Buddy. I smile coyly, no sense letting him know I'm studying him—where's the fun in that? And then I spot it. Big as day, a wedding band on his marriage finger.

BZZZZT!!!

The alerts blare in my subconscious mind! Immediate disqualification! Sure, he could be widowed or something, but if my experience has taught me anything; the easiest answer is usually the correct one. Too bad though, I could see myself giving him his money's worth if I were less inhibited. Morals are a curse in my line of work, to say the least, but I got 'em—and bad. This is just work after all. No different than a gig at Starbucks or Baby Gap—it pays the bills and when I'm ready to leave, I won't give this place a second thought. Compared to my childhood, doing so would be easy.

I retreat to the pole and hoist myself up to the top for the grand finale. Hanging upside down, I use my bra to tie my hands behind me. Then, slide slowly down head first, using only my toned thighs, to control my descent. I pretend like it's getting me off and the crowd goes wild. 'There, let's see any of these other Bitches do that!'

Truthfully, I've never much liked clubs. I'm not sure whether it's the overwhelming mixture of smoke, cologne, and cooked hair, the long lines in the ladies' room, or the crowds going into mosh-pit mode that sends my icky-meter into overdrive. All I know is, that something about it begins to press my anxiety button as soon as I step foot inside. Kinda the same way a drunk driver does with a police cruiser creeping up behind them.

Sure, I've been dragged to plenty of dives in my young life and I've even managed to have some decent times once I've got enough drinks in me, but that feeling is always there—lurking just beneath the surface. So where else would I choose to clock my thirty-hour work week? At a strip club? Trust me, the irony doesn't escape me.

Working in a Gentlemen's Club wasn't something I ever imagined for myself, either. I grew up in Frisco's upscale Pacific Heights district. I spent my youth shamelessly being pampered, thanks to my father's wealth. Private schooling, violin and piano lessons twice a week, which I loathed—international vacations, swanky galas, an Italian chef and maid were the staples of my upbringing. I was entitled to the best of the best and I was oblivious to the idea that anyone lived differently.

So, how does a girl born into affluence end up as an exotic dancer? It's pretty simple really. At an unusually young age, I fell head over heels in love with an infectious and sensual seductress called 'Dance'. I'm nothing without her—she defines me. We've been through everything together, literally. Even though she can be cruel at times, I just can't bring myself to give up on her, because I'm certain our passion for one another is mutual. To this day, she still has me sprung and I know she's going to show me the same devotion I've given her.

Quitting time finally arrives and as I walk through the main gallery on my way to the dressing room, I'm stopped by Monica. Monica Soto is a slim little Latina hottie with spiky short hair and delicate elfin features. She looks like she's sixteen, but you only have to stare into her sad brown eyes to understand she's already gone through more than most women twice her age. She acts like I'm her sister and although I have no idea why she'd choose me as a role model, I can't say I mind.

She's only been at the club for about a year. Before that, she was hard-core hooking for her crack-head douche of a Baby Daddy. His name is Punk in my book but I think I heard her call him Troy, once. Bastard; used to beat the shit out of her and then force himself on her 'til she got pregnant with her little boy, Eric. That little cutie saved her life. That and the fact that Punk ass OD'd about halfway through her pregnancy—there, now he's got a last name. Well, good riddance!

"Starr, Starr... guess what? I did it! I passed the test... I got my G.E.D!" she yelps at me. Monica reaches into her money pouch and pulls out a folded piece of paper which she unravels and hands to me. "Look!"

"Oh my God, Monica! I'm so proud of you, Mami... I knew you could do it!" I applaud.

Monica throws her arms around me, gushing: "Oh and plus, my Guidance Counselor, Mrs. Barlow, said she's gonna help me apply for financial aid soz I can go to Nursing School. Can you believe that; me a Nurse?"

"Of course, I can believe it, you worked your ass off sweetie... you deserve this. What do I always tell you?"

"The story of ME can only be written by ME," she recites. This was something Pappa always said, and I had adopted it as a part of my creed.

She grabs me again, this time so tight I have to take short breaths to keep from passing out. I hear her begin to sob as she pulls away: "I just want to thank you for everything you did for me and mi Hijo... damn, look at me, I'm such a cry baby, man..."

Someone thanking me isn't the norm, but I've learned to take all things in stride. "Hey, you did all the work," I commend.

Monica's face quickly turns to a question mark. "You leaving already?"

"Yeah girl, I'm outta here and not a second too soon, either."

"Okay, well, I'll call you later, let you know I made it home," she assures me.

Monica bounces off towards VIP.

My walk toward the staircase continues and I am again approached—this time by Mr. Wedding Band. He must have been lying in wait, eager to pounce. "Excuse me, sweet thing. Can I talk to you for a minute?"

I would say no if I thought it'd make any difference, but he's already into his pitch before I can part my lips. "I'm not sure if you recognize me from earlier, but anyway my name is Moses. It's a pleasure." He grabs my hand and kisses it, leaving me no choice in the matter. I notice he's removed his wedding ring—sneaky Bastard!

"I usually don't do anything like this, but I saw you and I had to let you know how beautiful I think you are," he continues. "So, what do you say we get out of here, huh? He smiles like he just kicked the game-winning field goal. The man licks his lips like a fake ass LL Cool J. Jeez, at least most guys come with some swagger.

My imagination conjures up a home where a perfect family waits on Daddy to return from a long day's work. There's a middle-of-the-road, Bible-belt wife who has no earthly idea where her husband spends both his nights and their money. Imagine the shock she'd feel if she could see him now. Then there are the children who adore and look up to this man—a smarmy loser that would rather spend his time making it rain on stranger's crotches than be with them. I know it shouldn't bother me because it's just the nature of men—but shit if it doesn't PISS ME OFF!

What can I do? Usually nothing; smile and ignore it. But tonight, I'm feeling extra ornery. I draw him closer, so I can whisper in his ear. "You know, maybe if you told your wife that more often, you wouldn't have to spend so much money here." He pulls away and looks at me, astonished. Part of me really wants to laugh, but I don't. I've done my good deed for the night.

The man quickly recovers and makes a straight line toward the exit. Another small heroic victory I dare not take credit for. I go downstairs feeling empty, as usual.

CHAPTER 3

BATTLE LINES

Home for me is a modest two-bedroom duplex on the Lower East Side of town just far enough away from the sights and sounds of the city. Not the sort of surroundings I grew up in, but I burned through my parents' money long ago, hiring private investigators to find their killers and bring them to justice.

I have to admit, the place reflects my personal artistic flair. The graffiti-inspired murals, to the gorgeous hardwood floors, and the floor-to-ceiling mirrors have transformed an extra room into my own personal studio. The rest of my furniture is as eclectic as my mood—a hodgepodge of flea market finds, antiques, and Danish Modern accents that somehow manage to co-exist in schizophrenic harmony.

Guys always ask me why a pretty young thing like me, lives alone. The truth is, I absolutely adore my solitude. I answer to no one. I can sleep until noon if I want without being jabbed in my back by some guy's weird little poker. I can work out in my studio without being harassed by pretentious 'roid-heads'. I eat whatever I want, whenever I want and I don't have to close the door to pooh. What else could a girl want?

I stand there, under the nozzle, and let the steaming water baste a night's worth of smoke and greasy dollar-bill residue off. Damn the water bills; I'll take an hour to bask in the steam if I feel like it. Shit, that's how long I need, to feel normal again.

I can't help but mentally rehash my earlier conversation with Deseree. Why did she have to bring all that shit up again? Just when I thought I'd regained some semblance of my sanity. The flashbacks of my parents' execution flicker in my mind like a grotesque movie trailer. Before long I feel a deep migraine make its way over my scalp and into my eyes until I'm seeing stars. Nothing a hit of that sticky icky can't cure.

This must be what the psychiatrists meant by Post-Traumatic-Stress. I remember getting a P.T.S.D. diagnosis on my college Psych evaluation before I dropped out—pompous idiots suggested I speak to someone about, my so-called Anger Issues—like I'm broken or some shit.

Needless to say, that made me Angry.

I swear they'll give out degrees to anyone nowadays. Regrettably, kicking that judgmental broad's stupid teeth in, landed me in hot water with the local PD and made it virtually impossible to get any sort of normal job. I still consider it an occupational hazard she should have been prepared for—but I guess her Medical Insurance company didn't agree.

I hop out, towel off, and wipe down the fogged mirror, so I can get a better look at God's blueprint for me. My thick curly hair spills down to the middle of my back. My breasts are perfect in my professional opinion—not too big or too small, with normal human-sized nipples—not those crazy big baby-feeders. You'd be shocked at some of the lazy titty bags that have pendulum'd their way through the doors at Eye Candy—tragic. Sir always defers to me for judgment and why not, I'm sort of an expert, if only from pure exposure.

I've been waxing my 'Precious' ever since high school. Truthfully, I don't even see the point of having hair anywhere but on my head. Maybe I just love the way things feel against bare skin—lotion, baby oil, water—even sweat. Oow and a man's hands—oh my God, there isn't anything like it!

Coating my skin in a rich mixture of body cream and baby oil before the moisture has a chance to escape my pores is a trade secret, I'd always watched my mother perform when I was a kid. I stand there glistening in the pale light of the candles I've lit. I know candles seem superfluous for an after-work shower, but hey, I need to relax any way I can, after dealing with so many dip shits on a nightly basis.

Entering my bedroom, I'm greeted by the familiar beep of an IM on my computer. It's from Candace, announcing that she's flying in from New York to visit soon and that she needs to be picked up from the airport.

You know how some friends call themselves Brothers or Sisters? Or Play-Cousins, whatever the hell that is? Well, Candace and I are truly kindred spirits. It's uncanny how we can finish each other's thoughts, like we share the same grey matter. From the first day we met in Mrs. Florentine's beginner's ballet class, we've been inseparable and I believe our connection even united our families.

It reminds me of an old Southern folk tale Pappa told me, about how there used to be only 'people' in the world before a cataclysm split them apart into two sexes. Supposedly that's why men and women always searched for that special someone, forever after. Each is seeking to reconnect with their 'Split Apart', as soul mates are called in the story. In my case, I'm certain my Split Apart was then split apart again—it's the only explanation for the intensity of my relationship with Candace!

My Pappa; was an Eagle in high-end Real Estate and her Dad, a brilliant Contractor. They quickly became necessary to one another, creating a lasting bond. Our mothers enjoyed a twin passion for shopping, fashion, and gossip. They spent their days chattering relentlessly about who showed up where, wearing what—and why that was a mistake. Shared meals, family outings, and sleepovers were a regular occurrence between the Tibbaduax's and Smith's. Who could've foreseen that the close bond forged by two children would eventually end in a Greek tragedy triple homicide?

It seems, Pappa and Mr. Smith's business put them in contact with a lot of affluent people, and unfortunately, not all of them had acquired their wealth legally. The rest, as they say, is cosmic fate. From what the cops were able to tell us, some sort of business deal involving a very profitable piece of land—, that was supposed to house the new Oakland Raiders Stadium, went south. This was the type of deal that would've generated billions in profit for the landowner.

Candace and her mom were out of town when Mr. Smith was murdered and they were unharmed. Mrs. Smith or Deb, as I was instructed to call her—she took me in and raised us like sisters. She would introduce us as her lovely daughters, and enter us in all sorts of pageants. I honestly felt like a princess.

After losing my parents I never thought I would feel complete again—but there it was, almost perfect. Right up until our sophomore year of high school, when years of Hypertension and Diabetes finally caught up with Deb and she suffered a major stroke. At least, that was the official diagnosis.

Some experts believe talking is CRITICAL after a traumatizing event. They coaxed Candace to spill her proverbial beans all over the place. In the end, all she got was an anxiety complex. Me on the other hand, I'm the kind of girl who sees silence as the only way to swim through pain and survive. I adore Candace for understanding that and not pushing me.

Shortly After the stroke landed Mrs. Smith in an assisted living place, Candace got snatched away, to live with her equally rich relatives in New York. So, here I am thinking we're gonna become part of Manhattan's regal class. Of course, they had no interest in taking my teenaged ass along. We were separated—her into high society, me into the cramped long-beach apartment of my Aunt and Uncle-in-law. Stuffed wall to wall with ratty old furniture, air mattress beds, and linoleum tile floors—you would have thought this urban eyesore would have finally humbled me—it didn't. So, I quadrupled down on my babysitting hustle, and as soon as I hit the legal emancipation age, I was outta there!

Candace and I lost touch as impetuous youngsters do; when dealing with the angst of adult challenges. We were eventually able to reconnect, with the advent of My-Space and Facebook, however now, we're two dramatically altered souls. Now, with this upcoming visit—our first in many years—I'm faced with a tremendous problem. What if she finds out the truth about the new me?

I confirm Candace's pick-up instructions and log off. My screensaver, a photo of Candace and me at a childhood recital, pops onto the monitor. I stare at our young faces, so innocent and carefree. I wonder if she'd understand why things had to be this way.

That this is the only option I have to hold on to my life's dream? That a strip club is the only place that would pay someone like me to dance. And, what about my bone-chilling secret? Would she ever be able to forgive my betrayal? Or understand that I lied to protect her from the unbearable truth behind her father's death? Sure, Deb had conjured up quite a believable explanation—but I had played a starring role in the deceit.

So, what now? Should I tell Candace at all, or just continue to pretend like I was caught under the same cloud of misinformation as she'd been? Either way, I know this isn't just a minor infraction. This will be life-changing—the kind of treachery that will put our friendship to the ultimate test and rewrite the terms of this association.

Unbeknownst to me, the Asian Prosperity Foundation is hosting a luxury gala across town the following day. A sizable banquet hall has been stuffed with businesspeople for the annual celebration of Asian culture, pride, and achievement. It's also an excuse to network with the most powerful leaders in the city.

Billionaire Mogul, Nu Dinh, founder of Dinh Technologies is the guest of honor. Still spry and imposing in his late sixties, he sits at the head of a banquet table flanked by his two, twenty-something sons, Quan and Lanh.

Nu Dinh is an enigma of sorts. In addition to being a dynamic businessman, and shrewd tactician he is also a Holy-man. A Thai immigrant, Nu arrived in America in the early 80s and immediately set to cultivating his false persona as a charitable peacemaker. On the other side of the coin, Nu heads one of the most vicious crime syndicates ever to reach US soil—an organization known as the Yukoshi Clan.

I know it sounds typical but make no mistake, these guys aren't to be taken lightly. In addition to controlling all illegal gambling and racketeering in San Francisco, Nu's tribe has also gotten their hands elbow-deep into prostitution, money laundering, grand larceny, smuggling, weapons, and narcotics—oh, and let us not forget—murder. Yukoshi's atrocities are the stuff of legends and nightmares in the criminal underworld!

His children are spectacles to be marveled at. The oldest boy, Quan, is a handsome clone of his father, possessing all the charm, wisdom, and business savvy you might expect from a man born into the Dinh family. A brilliant Stanford Law Grad, he was expected to devote his life to upholding the laws of the U.S. Constitution—but let's be honest, that sounds incredibly boring.

Fiercely loyal to Family and Creed, he chose instead to focus his knowledge of Legal Statutes and Congressional palm-greasing towards the expansion of the Dinh Dynasty at all costs.

Younger brother, Lanh is an effete bleach-blonde hipster poser. But his looks belie his actions—which are those of a dangerous sociopath. At the flip of a switch, he can go from quiet and methodical to extremely impulsive; prone to fits of rage and life-threatening outbursts of violence.

He is the perfect 'muscle' for the Dinh family empire, but he's just as often a liability to their public image. Lanh's troubles with the law and his many addictions frequently land him in hot water.

Lanh however, is only a middle child. Nu Dinh also has a beloved daughter, named Mao Lei. She provides the much-needed sea of calm for her turbulent family. She too is devoted to her father and she manages to smooth out any rivalries between her brothers. Mao Lei knows what goes on behind the scenes, but she's above all that and has chosen to focus on the finer Business points at hand. In a way, I don't blame her. I know what it means to lose family and I probably would do the same thing to keep mine together.

At the banquet, a small mousey woman makes her way to the podium to introduce the man of the hour.

"...His Technology, Construction, and Agricultural contributions have generated over six billion dollars in development for San Francisco's Asian Communities."

Blah, blah, blah, whatever, sweetheart. You know everyone is only here to kiss Nu Dinh's skinny ass and get drunk off of complementary Saki. She continues: "So... without further ado, may I present the winner of The NAAAP Business Man of the Year Award, Mr. Nu Dinh!" The room erupts in a standing ovation. Nu Dinh takes the stage, genuinely bashful about all the applause.

"Thank you, thank you. It is a privilege to accept such an honor. Like so many of you who hail from the Southern hemisphere, I am daily forced to pause and reflect on how miraculously we have managed to achieve the immigrant's dream in our wonderful, adopted country. I'd like to thank everyone that has supported me throughout these long years. First and foremost, my beloved sons, Quan and Lanh..."

Quan raises his glass, graciously saluting his father. Lanh, stands to accept the applause for himself, holding up the empty bottle he's just drained.

"Also, I wish to thank my daughter, Mao Lei.

They cheer, but she is not in attendance. Mao Lei should be here right now, but she's in Beijing managing crucial trade talks. Yes... I am truly a proud father."

After several more names, Nu regales his audience with a colorful story from his youth.

Along the length of the tables in the cavernous banquet hall, most listen with respect, and adoration but a few let their attention drift to the serving platters of food set out nearby. There is enough here, to feed the impoverished villages from which most of them fled. Piles of fried prawns, the freshest sushi, and vegetables preserved crisp in a variety of delicate sauces. Old hungers that can never be satisfied take their grip on these guests.

At that very moment, the classically lovely, Mao Lei arrives at the San Francisco International Airport. She's been thirty hours in the air but still looks fresh as a newly picked daisy. She intends to surprise her father at his banquet. Mao Lei is met by her personal escort while she's still wrapped up in a very private, very personal phone conversation with her father's number one lackey, Daygo Jin.

Well, to be fair Daygo is not just a lackey—this man surprised Mao Lei by being handsome, ambitious, and unassumingly smart. Mao Lei has been **50 SHADES OF BONING** him for close to a year now behind her father's back. Now, she assures him, "Yes, everything went well. The partners adored my presentation... I had those old fools practically eating out of my hands."

Mao Lei giggles at his crude joke. "How did I know you would say that?"

As the two escorts grab her bags, Mao Lei works diligently to disguise the ruse in front of her handlers. She exits the airport behind the men and is led to a large SUV. One of the men opens the door and lets the preoccupied young lady in.

"Well, I'm not sure I'll be able to meet you tonight. My father will be hovering... perhaps tomorrow..."

The man shuts the door behind her, then takes the driver's seat while his partner loads Miss Thing's bags into the trunk. Mao Lei kicks her feet up on the seat and removes her shoes. The pig of a driver adjusts his rear-view mirror to look at her. Visibly annoyed, she quickly raises the privacy window but he can still hear her sweet and lusty tone, "Mmm, that sounds wonderful. Okay, I'll see you soon. Love you too!" She seductively bites her lip at the thought of another dangerous romp with her Soldier Prince.

Back at the NAAAP Gala, Daygo stands apart from the crowd and reluctantly ends his call. He returns to mingle but many shy away from him. Daygo is a fierce warrior, carved from pure steal and charged with maintaining the Dinh Security Network. He understands that; Nu has his little princess earmarked for someone else, but he doesn't care. She is his one weakness.

As Mao Lei's ride readies to depart the airport, two black sedans screech to a halt on the side of it. Several Latino gang members jump out, brandishing automatic weapons. They gun down the driver and other helper then yank the kicking, screaming Mao Lei out. Then they speed off with the young lady in tow—an abduction accomplished in under a minute, or so Channel 5 reports. These back-and-forth attacks on the part of San Francisco's crime families have become a common occurrence. Shoot-outs, bombings, and assassinations have disrupted the entire city—and the kidnapping of Nu Dinh's only daughter will most certainly inspire swift and ferocious retaliation.

The silky high cheekbones and full lips of Isreal St. Claire draw close to her phone, to answer an incoming call. As brilliant as she is beautiful, Isreal is an Italian American mob lieutenant who at only thirty, already has 61 confirmed high-profile kills to her credit. On the other end; the hair-covered muzzle of her commander. She doesn't know his real name, so she simply calls him Boss and has come to think of him as her 'Financier'. The man's deep voice bares a distinct raspy Caribbean resemblance that flows out smooth like Bourbon.

"The package has been acquired in good condition, Boss," she reports.

"Guh. Mek sir ih stays dat weh," the grouchy voice replies.

"As you wish." Isreal ends the call with her benefactor, removes the memory card, and methodically grinds the phone into dust under her thin stiletto boot heel before climbing into her Dark-Grey Ferrari F12 McLaren and disappearing into the haze of the night.

CHAPTER 4

FAMILIAR GHOSTS

Another night of being eye-raped by socially inept weirdos is almost over. As I sit there, half-listening to the absurd ramblings of some counterfeit tattooed, chucky-cheesy, gold-toothed, junior-thug rapper wanna-be, a single thought reverberates inside my skull: "There's just got to be a better way."

"... I'm just sayin' though, it's my birthday, Mami. You can't give a Playa a little thrill? Com'on and blow out this candle." His breath reeks and my eyes can't roll back far enough to demonstrate my disinterest. Cold silence is wasted on him. Seriously, it's as if all the dudes of my generation have lost their ability to hold a normal conversation. You wouldn't believe some of the lines these jackasses trot out.

'No wonder I'm single.'

"You see this chain?" The Birthday Boy grabs one of the gold-plated chains on his neck and holds it up so close to my face, that I can smell the spray paint—I've had it!

"Aww, that's so cute... my little cousin got one just like that when he turned Big 6," I tell him.

"Haha, real funny, Hoe. I'm about to sign with Terror Squad Music." He waggles his free-styling' dick inside his baggy sweatpants. "You better get this while it still can be got."

'Did this lame chump just call me a Hoe? Looks like I'm going back to jail tonight!'

His Homies snicker and I feel my face heat up and my fist clinch. I check for backup and spy two of our larger bouncers close by. I prepare to deliver a right-cross, but just before I can strike, I catch a glance at the clock. Suddenly, all of the malice I feel, cools. Lucky for this punk, it's quitting time. I dare not miss my escape for this dude.

I smile at the little A-hole instead. "Yeah freak, I thought that would change your uppity-ass attitude. So, why don't you show me that monkey?" he continues, oblivious.

"Well, Daddy, I tell you what... you go sign your deal, then your broke ass can buy as many monkeys as you want... Fuckin clown!"

His friends explode with laughter, but I'm halfway to the dressing room before he's able to shake off the verbal mud I just flung in his face.

"Yo, fuck you, Bitch! You ain't shit but a high-priced hooker anyway," Birthday Boy shouts. "Man, screw this place... let's go!" His buddies follow him out, still laughing and cracking on him.

On my way to the locker room, I spot an eerily familiar face—not that I recognize him or anything, but for the fact that he's been dry-staring at me from the bar all night. From what I can tell he hasn't said a word to anyone but the Bartender—let alone, accepted a dance. He's handsom-ish I guess, from what I can see of him beneath the shadow of his fedora—but even handsome can be crazy, haven't you seen Dexter? Besides, what kind of person sits in a place like this all-night eye stalking chicks—an axe murderer, that's what kind.

As I move passed him, "Excuse me, Miss... I need to speak to you," the man says in a cultured slightly foreign, almost fatherly tone.

I don't break my stride. "Sorry sweetie, I'm off the clock," I blurt, a trick I learned early on in this business. When the clock strikes, keep your head down and your feet moving. That's when Princes start turning into Niggas and Niggas start changing back to Frogs.

And then—

"JEADDA NICOLE TIBBADAUX!!!" he roars. The howl of his draconian voice cuts through the smoggy air like an arrow halting my hasty exit. All at once, it hits me like a bag of bricks—that voice, that damned voice! I slowly turn to face the man now silhouetted in smoke, and as he glares at me; I quickly realize where I recognize him from.

"You... it's you!" is all I can murmur, as panic takes hold of my throat like an abusive Ex-boyfriend. It's him! After all these years, he's found me! My childhood Boogie-man; the one responsible for my mother's agonizing end—and the bastard who sealed my father's fate with a simple nod of his head. He's come to finish the job!

I rush downstairs, stride for my locker, and fling it open—diving into my purse for my cell. I'm shaking, but I manage to call our head bouncer, Keith. Keith used to play Line-Backer for the Niners until he got kicked out of the league for conduct unbecoming or some crazy shit like that. He used to come into the club and boo-hoo on my shoulder. I couldn't help but agree that the decision to expel him reeked of hypocrisy and yes, a bit of racism. I mean banishing a man for being too brutal in the NFL is kind of like, judging a stray mut for sniffing tail.

"They don't ban Hockey players from attacking one another in all-out brawls now do they?" he would lobby. Now Keith employs his special brand of head-busting in the disbursement of unruly customers. Keith answers and I hear him trying to holler at one of the dancers. "Keith... help me!" I shout.

"Who dis?" he answers.

"Keith... it's me, Jeadda."

"Keith don't know no Jeadda," he explains, staring at his phone like he's expecting a picture to appear.

"It's Starr, fool!"

"Oh, what up girl?"

I rummage deeper inside my purse and pull out a small canister of pepper spray, while I continue talking. "Keith, there's somebody up there trying to get me... I need you to guard the dressing room so I can get out." My voice rises in panic.

"What's he look like?" Keith chirps.

"I dunno... He's at the Bar, fancy hat guy", I bark.

Upstairs, Keith scans the Main Room and sees the man still seated at the bar with a fixed gaze on the stairs. "Don't trip, Babe, I see him... I'll bust him up good for you," he vows.

"No, wait! Keith... he's a—"

Too late—Keith's already hung up and is headed towards the bar. He advances on the man from behind. "Hey, buddy... time to go!" he rumbles. The man at the bar cocks his head so he can see who's interrupting him. Unimpressed, he ignores the command, which is just the sort of response a knuckle-dragger like Keith is hoping for. Keith grins at the perceived disrespect, savoring the thrashing he plans to administer.

He grabs the man's shoulder. "I said, it's time to go, Mother Fucker!" Without warning and as swift as a bolt of lightning, the man brings an elbow down neatly shattering Keith's humerus like a breadstick. Keith screams in agony, so I guess that shit wasn't so humorous after all—'oh forget ya'll, you don't know what's funny'.

Anywho, more bouncers rush to Keith's aid, but most stop short after the man dispatches two of them with Brazilian jiu-jitsu moves. In all the melee, I'm able to quietly slip out a side door, to the staff parking lot.

Outside, I am battered by the frigid winter wind. I've forgotten my coat and I nearly fall during the race to my car. Forcing my keys into the lock of my Mustang, I crank the heat and zoom off out of the lot. By this time, the other guards have conceded and stepped aside allowing the dark stranger to casually exit the club.

Now in the relative enclosure of my baby, I finally feel safe. My Ex, the same one that gave me the mace, insisted I let him make some upgrades on her as soon as we pulled out of the dealership. So now, I drive one of the fastest, meanest little rockets on the streets. Sweet right? Well, if he sounds like Prince Charming don't be fooled, it was all just his way of controlling me. Asshole loaded this thing with Tech but refused to teach me how to use any of it, so I'd keep him around. Shiiiit, guess he forgot about Google. The insecure little buster had even low-jacked my ass in the process!

As I streak toward home, I notice a dark-colored SUV with tinted windows trailing me—strange for this time of night. I'm used to having the roads to myself and can cruise to my Old-School playlist. I make a right turn and the SUV follows. Two more rights and he stays on my tail. 'Alright, Ass-hole let's see how you feel about Turbo!' I pound the petal.

BEEEEEEP!

The low fuel gauge beeps scaring me halfway into the back seat. "Damn it, you've gotta be kidding me right now", I scold. There's no way I'm going to make it home from here on 'E'. Luckily, I spot a well-lit 24-hour gas station with several loitering patrons in the parking lot. I quickly cut in and the dark truck continues passed me. Now, I get to wonder, if I was actually being followed, or if my paranoia is just getting out of hand. I pull up to the pump at the far end of the station and glance over at a group of men, standing by their cars on the other side of the lot. They must be having a beats contest or something I assume by the bass-pumping music I hear. Still a tad unsettled, I put my sweat shirt and skull cap on—no need to attract any undue attention at this time of night, in this part of town.'

I have to say that at this moment, I am relieved by the convenience of the 'PAY AT THE PUMP' option. Of course, technology is not without its irony and I'm treated to a harsh jolt of it, when I swipe my card. The damn thing beeps at me like I've just answered a question wrong on Family Feud. It generates a message: ERROR PAY

INSIDE—Wonderful. I stride toward the convenience store, trying my best to look like I belong.

Inside, I get in line behind two Hispanic guys, day laborers obviously, by their paint-splashed pants and work boots. Just as I attempt to shake off some of my apprehension, I hear voices at the back of the store.

"Dog, I promise she was gobbling my shit so hard, I thought the bitch was gonna suck my soul out!"

Although; I've become accustomed to such exchanges in my line of work, it still grinds on my nerves. Bitches and Hoes, Tricks and Sluts—alright, we get it already! Expand your damn vocabulary fellas!

"I told you Felisha's a freak, Cuz," another man laughs.

A cloud of thick smoke floats passed my head. They pause and my ears rise like an old bloodhound. Suddenly, I can feel their eyes examining me. "Yo, peep game," one of them alerts the other.

"Daaaamn!" his friend agrees.

This body is a gift and a curse. The older Hispanic man glances back at me and I read concern in his tired eyes. To my disappointment, they pay for their items and leave, unwilling or unable to get involved.

The thugs saddle up behind me, uncomfortably close.

"Twenty on twelve," I say, handing the attendant my card.

He's a small man—I can't count on him either.

"Hey Girl, what you doing out here so late," one of the men whispers over my shoulder. Eww, his breath is a definite problem. I ignore him.

"Hey! My boy's talking to you!" the other man insists, yanking the hat off of my head. I turn around and my heart jumps into my throat as I recognize the same young thug I insulted back at the club. His mouth curls into an ominous smirk as clearly, he recognizes me too. His friend's smile is mean. "Check it, bro, it's that little dick-tease from the club."

"Oh shit, you right, Cuz," his friend confirms.

"I think you still owe me a little something," the Birthday Boy says. Just then the cashier returns with my card. His eyes suggest I run and I take the hint, squeezing between the men to make my retreat.

Headed back to the car, I can't help but wonder if it's worth the risk to just haul ass on empty. One glance at the pitch-black stretch of highway, tells me it's not. I jam the nozzle in and begin to pump, but the gas is flowing absurdly slow.

Just then, the men emerge from the store. Thug-friend quickly spots me and points me out to Birthday Boy. Before I know it, they box me in by the pump.

"Say 'Hoe, what you think me and my boy can get for a dollar", friend quizzes.

"Man, fuck that, I ain't paying this Freak shit... she owes me! Ain't that right, Freak?" Birthday Boy demands.

I see now, this is gonna have to get physical. I grip my keys and lace them between my fingers like wolverine claws. "Look, I don't want any trouble fellas, okay?"

"AYE, WHAT THE HELL IS YOU FOOLS DOIN?" a voice bellows from across the lot. Moments later, I am surrounded by a mob of degenerates. They snicker and leer at me and I catch myself wondering if it's just a coincidence that these are all men of color. One of them looks like he could even be a close relative—someone I'd be introduced to at my next family reunion as a second cousin or some shit. The others are characters straight out of a John Singleton movie. I want to cry out, 'You are supposed to be my brothers! You should be protecting me!'

My instinct for self-preservation cuts in, flashing a warning as clear as the gas pump message: 'STOP IT JEADDA... THERE'S NO TIME FOR THAT SHIT NOW—THIS IS HAPPENING, LIKE IT OR NOT!' I remember my pepper spray. I'll have to douse the entire area, but at least I'll get all the vermin!

I continue to plead with them while furtively searching my pocket for the small canister. Before I can grab it, one of them locks onto my arm and another clamps his hand down over my mouth. They rip the clothes from my body like tissue paper and the raw cold air shocks my skin causing me to go berserk. I flail and kick out in all directions, managing to score some lucky shots until my rebellion is ceased by a mind-numbing jolt of pain. Some coward has slammed his fist into the back of my head, and my body crumples.

"Hurry up and put that bitch in the trunk!" I hear Birthday Boy yell, but his voice sounds tiny and far away. I feel myself being hoisted up and tossed like a sack of potatoes into a cold, metal trunk.

"What we gonna do with her?" one of the accomplices asks.

"Shit she's a stripper... what AIN'T we gonna do with her?" Birthday Boy chuckles.

They share a group laugh that stops short with the sound of screeching tires and a car door opening. I can only pray the store cashier called the police. If they saved me, it might just change my opinion of 'Cops' in general. Instead, I hear a voice—more like a hazy echo of a voice.

"Gentlemen, I don't think you wanna do that."

They slam the lid over me and although the smell of gas and rubber is nauseating, I can't even move let alone vomit.

"Fuck off, pops! This ain't got nothing to do with you!" someone yells.

Silence...

Then he says, "I got no beef with you fellas. But I can't let you take her, I need her."

"Shit, we need her too, get the next one mutha fucka!"

"You don't understand."

CLICK—the sound of a pistol being cocked.

"I UNDERSTAND YOU BETTER GET THE FUCK OUTTA HERE BEFORE I BLOW NOODLES OUT YOUR HEAD, PUNK!!!"

I lie in the trunk thinking, 'Holy shit, whoever this guy is, he's brave! I hope his macho shit doesn't get both our asses killed. I try to speculate who would be crazy enough to risk his neck for me, but I draw all blanks.

"Okay, if you insist..." My would-be rescuer sounds calm, and resolute.

Next, I hear the meaty exchange of fists grinding into faces accompanied by grunts of pain as precision strikes are thrown and absorbed—The unmistakable thud of bodies getting tossed around. I hear them land hard on the wet pavement.

—SMACK! KA-POW! SLAM!

Inside the trunk, all I can do is hope they aren't beating the breaks off my hero. It's killing me not to see what's happening. Will I be violently raped or valiantly rescued?

Next—

Silence—except for the pounding inside my chest. The door to my steel tomb flies open; splashing blinding light into my eyes. I can only see a giant blur hovering over me: "No, please NO!" an annoyingly feeble voice blares. The sounds of quiet sobs fill my ears as massive arms lift me and carry me away passed many prone bodies being dusted by light rain. I hope one of them is the Birthday Boy—serves him right for putting his ashy little hands on me. "It's okay, you're safe now. Let's get you outta here," the voice hums as I struggle to remain conscious. Just before blacking out, I finally realize it is me who was crying that whole time.

CHAPTER 5

CURIOSITY KILLS

The sun is setting. Its last rays find my face, harshly waking me from the most comfortable sleep I've had in months. I open my eyes to see a window framed by old-fashioned flower curtains and immediately know I'm somewhere I shouldn't be. Sitting up, I find myself in a small, trim room. The last thing I remember is being carried off into the night by a giant shadow blob wearing musky sweet cologne. 'Where the hell am I?' my mind screams at me.

Touching the throbbing knot on my forehead confirms my dream was no dream at all—my capture is real and evidently still in progress. An attempt to stand on my own proves futile as I plummet to the floor. I stay there, listening for any signs that I've been detected. The door is closed—but is it locked? Dragging myself back up on the bed, I breathe deep to catch my bearings.

The walls of my room are filled with military awards, pictures, and other honors. 'What kind of kidnapper is this?' Then... one photo sends shock waves through my body. I realize I'm not in the home of any petty thug. Somehow, I've made my way into the Devil's lair—the strange man watching me from the bar—my father's killer! My heart struggles to break out of my rib cage and the walls close in. I try getting up again and can make it to the window this time. There, I look out at a two-story drop that, even if I survived it, would leave me severely hobbled.

I glance back over my shoulder at the wall—so many medals—so many honors. How can a man be a ruthless villain and a respected military hero at the same time? He looks happy in the pictures; many of which show him with his arms around what must be his devoted companion. So, what happened to him? What made him the butcher of innocent families?

My imagination hops aboard the crazy train. He must be some kind of disgraced veteran charged with horrible war crimes that resulted in his dishonorable discharge. Unleashed into an unsuspecting society, he went on the warpath.

Truth is, none of it matters now. I am stuck in this place and if I ever want to get out alive, I have to do something! My instincts compel me to grab a weapon. 'Ooow... one of these nice big trophies would be perfect!' I practice swinging it around.

Suddenly, the sound of footsteps creaking on the stairs snatches my attention. I dive back into bed and hide my weapon beneath the blankets. After what seems like ages the door eases open. I hold the trophy tight and wait for my captor to come within arm's length.

Then, I'm distracted by another sound—the clinking of metal against glass as he gently sets a tray down on the table by the bed. Curiosity wars with my fear as I inhale the fresh, tangy scent of lemon tea.

My eyes are still squeezed shut and I try not to flinch when a cool, damp cloth is placed on my forehead. He says in a stern tone: "I would prefer it, if you didn't hit me with that. I'm quite fond of that one."

I slowly open my eyes, just in time to see the hulking man sink into a rocking chair facing the bed. Setting my weapon on the nightstand I ask, "What are you going to do with me?"

He leans back and sips from a mug. "Do with you? I'm not going to do anything with you."

"So why did you bring me here?"

"You would have preferred to be left in the trunk?" he asks and I can't tell if his sarcasm is meant to interject levity or what, but this seriously isn't the time or place for jokes.

"Your father... he was a good man. He did not deserve what happened to him. None of you did." His words stab me like a hundred knives. I clench my knees to my chest as tears begin to well my eyes.

How dare he speak about my father to me! I know I'm in no position to demand an explanation but I can't stop myself. "Then why... why did you let them kill him? You just sat there, smoking that damned cigar!"

His eyes widen, but he recovers quickly. "I understand. You have years of hatred built up inside of you. Haunted by the memory of a monster. But despite how things may appear, I can assure you, I am not the man you seek." he replies.

'Liar!' I wish I could say it out loud, but the last thing I want to do is set this guy off. And so, I commit myself wholly to the arduous task of tongue-biting.

"My name is Luther Cofaxx. First Lieutenant Luther James Cofaxx, U.S. Marine Corps.—and I am not your villain, Jeadda. He leans forward out of the shadows. "But I can help you find him."

I just don't know what to think. My head is pounding. He continues, to take my silence as acceptance and so he continues to clarify.

"The man you want is called Dunlock, but I know him by his given name, Di Tiaay Asensea. I have been hunting him for nearly twelve years now and every time I get close, he disappears underground again. Dunlock is a killer, a drug lord, and one of the most dangerous men in the world." He sighs and drops his gaze. "... and he is my brother."

This S.O.B must think I've got a concussion to risk telling such an outrageous story. It's insulting. "I know this may sound unbelievable to you Jeadda, but before your father's death, he agreed to help us bring Dunlock down. I think that's why he was murdered."

"My father... help you?" I scoff.

"I was with the S.F.P.D. at the time. We were set to infiltrate T.R.A.P. through a real-estate deal. Your father was just supposed to set up a deal... that should have been the beginning and end of his involvement. He was happy to lend a hand to protect this city... to protect the innocence of children, like you."

"Oh, let me guess, now you're gonna tell me something went horribly wrong?" I roll my eyes.

"No, I'm going to tell you it's my fault. He shouldn't have been there... he wasn't ready. I made a mistake," he says.

"What do you want from me?" I demand.

"I want you to help me bring Dunlock to justice."

That arrogant prick! Who does he think he is? I want to punch him right in his face.

I'm no fool, I keep telling myself. My father didn't trust cops any more than I do, and with good reason. As a young boy he had seen his fair share of police corruption. He used to say that a Crooked Cop was an Oxymoron.

'Happy to lend a hand? Pu-lease! Are we even talking about the same man'.

"What makes you think I would help you... or even believe you?", I assert.

"Forgive me... I just assumed you would want the men responsible for your parent's murder to pay." He rises to his feet. "You are free to go whenever you wish... but make no mistake, Dunlock is still out there and if he isn't stopped, you will never be safe. He will hunt you and he WILL find you... just as I did."

Cofaxx turns to leave but as he reaches the door, he pauses. "I'm extremely sorry for your loss," he says. He heads downstairs leaving the door open.

I remain in bed stewing over the Fantasmic tale I've just heard—it stank like rotten Swiss-cheese and had far more holes in it. My eye catches the steam wafting from the other cup of liquid and I breathe in the aroma. Time for one of those crossroads" decisions. "Well, if he wanted to poison me, why bother with a bedtime story," I wager. I gulp the tea down.

Several minutes later I'm at the bottom of the stairs, within staring distance of the front door. I know I should leave but I've somehow become intrigued by this Cofaxx guy's so-called opportunity for revenge. What kind of mind fuck was that?"

I glance across at the living room to the right of me. There are definite signs of a feminine influence. More framed photographs depict a loving and happy couple. But the furniture is dated and I see the bachelor's mess of a man who's been falling asleep on the couch lately, scattered throughout. Where is she now? Has his obsession with this Dunlock character, driven her away?"

The soothing drawl of an old-school ballad coming from the back of the house pulls me there. My stomach rumbles as I inhale the scent of Seafood Gumbo in the atmosphere and long-forgotten memories wash over me. I recall how my father, a total Cajun cliché, loved dishing it up for every holiday. This smells spicy and rich, just like Pappa's recipe.

I peek around the kitchen doorway like a timid feral cat to find my host, busy at the stove in a frilly woman's apron while he stirs the contents of a huge pot. 'What kind of killer does this? No killer at all.' Another crossroads decision—one that apparently my stomach has already made for me. As if reading my mind, and without ever giving any clue that he notices me, he advises, "You should probably eat something before you go. You've been asleep for more than twenty-four hours."

Cofaxx holds out a steaming bowl. "And I would enjoy the company," he admits.

I ease cautiously towards him to accept it. "The men that attacked me... what happened to them?" I ask.

"Those boys just needed to be taught some manners. They won't be bothering you anymore." He hands me a spoon.

I take a seat at his table—the one closest to his back door, of course. Cofaxx sits opposite me. "Be careful, it's still hot," he warns. Before he can say grace, I begin to shovel spoonfuls of the delicious stew into my mouth quickly finishing and slurping the last drops of juice from the bowl.

Cofaxx stares curiously at my reaction. Amazing how fast I just threw six years of etiquette classes out the window. He might as well have poured it into a pig trough. Awkward isn't even the word for what I feel, but I refuse to show it. "So… you're a cop?" I deflect.

"I don't really know what I am anymore."

"So, how do we get this Dunlock?"

His dark eyes glint. "First, you need to get your strength back." He slides his bowl of Gumbo in front of me.

I frown. And then I eat. We speak for hours about my father - the Mission he had supposedly participated in, and the Sirens, some elite fighting squad of which he said I could be a part; if I was so inclined. By the end of our conversation, I still don't exactly trust him—however, I find I no longer want to punch his face—now that's progress.

CHAPTER 6

MIDDLE MEN

Not even a week later, I'm back at the club—as if I haven't learned my lesson at all. I stare at my reflection in the dressing room mirror thinking, "What the hell are you doing back here?" I'm covered in bruises and my shades barely hide my freshly dotted eye—thank goodness I have my sweats on.

The other dancers pay little attention to me, but I know there's no way my damage will go ignored by the hawks upstairs. Cheeks jangles what's left of my nerves with her shrill voice.

"I don't give a damn what that little Mu-Fucka say! Let his midget ass get up on the pole if he thinks it's so damn easy, cuz I ain't doin' it! Some bitches ain't built for all that shit!" she screeches.

Cheeks careens around a corner followed by two of her minions and stops at my locker. "Ya'll go ahead," she tells Thing 1 and 2 and they clomp off chewing their gum cud like the stupid cows they are. "Hey Starr... you gotta comb, girl? Some stupid ass got crumbs all in my hair... Fat Bastard!" she complains removing her wig.

I hand her a comb while trying to avoid eye contact. She quickly rakes the crumbs out of the dead, synthetic mop that passes for her wig and tries to hand back my ruined comb. Her eyes challenge me to take it.

"Nah, girl, you keep it. I have tons of those," I insist. Suddenly, she snatches the oversized shades off my face, exposing my injuries. "Girl, what the hell happened to you?" She doesn't even attempt to sound concerned.

"Cheeks Damn! It's nothing... I just fell."

"Fell... on whose fist?" she shrieks.

"Look, like I said, it's nothing... really!" I set my stunner shades carefully back into place.

"Well, you better not let Lil' Man see that NOTHING! Mmm hmm, he ain't gonna like that shit."

Cheeks turns on her platforms and I realize that no matter how ghetto she may be, she's right—Sir is definitely going to have a shit fit if he sees this. I have to force myself to go up the stairs.

The club is busy, especially for a Tuesday. As I make my way through the crowd, I spot Sir Mont'e near the bar, holding court with a few B-list celebrity-type friends of his.

I lower my head and pick up the pace, but Nikki, one of the newer cocktail waitresses, crashes smack into me. Her drinks take flight and I'm certain Sir notices it. I envision a calculator clicking away inside his head, deducting the cost of floored drinks from her paycheck. "Oh my God I'm so sorry, are you okay?" Nikki erupts in frantic apology.

"I'm fine, don't worry about it." I can feel Sir Mont'e creeping up directly behind me. I don't know how he does it—he must be half Leprechaun, which would also explain his height or lack thereof.

"What the hell... is wrong with you?" He looks me up and down the way a Pimp might examine a damaged Filly from his stable.

"What?" That's all I can think to say.

He whips off my glasses. "Your face, Nigga that's what! What the hell is wrong with your face?" He manages to make it sound like something that happened to ***him***.

"Sir, can we talk about this some other time? I'm really not feeling well right now," I plead.

"Oh, I'm sorry, I had no idea you were under the weather. Tell you what, I can help with that: Look over there at that sign for me. What does it say?"

The blinking neon sign taunts me as I read, "Sir Mont'e Presents Club Eye Candy," I recite.

"Oh okay, and who am I?" he asks in a prissy manner.

"Sir," I reply.

"Sir what?"

"Sir Mont'e Money Bags."

"Sir Mont'e Mother-fuckin' Money Bags, you God damn right! And this is MY club, and you are MY employee, which means you don't get to walk through MY main room lookin' like a hot mess and tell me not to worry about the shit! I sell candy—not beat-up ass excuses!

At this point, he's literally hopping up and down and I have to bite my tongue to keep from laughing. He's about as threatening as an angry hamster. "Yes, Sir," I murmur, knowing full well that he's just talking to hear himself preen.

"I don't know what the hell you buckets is thinking!

He pauses to think of some other way I might still be useful.

You know what, on second thought... take your broke-down ass home!" All he needs is for everyone to believe the idea is his own to save some face. For all his bark, he genuinely cares. As I turn to exit, he calls out after me. "Hey, Starr? Call me if you need anything, Mmm-kay?" he says.

"Thanks, Sir."

I blow him a kiss and he waves me off, like the big Brother figure, he is. As I leave, I wonder if Eye Candy is the only club in town that boasts our very own Soft hearted-Keebler-Pimp.

At that very moment, across town at a Mission District Trap House, Latino gang leader, Cisco has just returned from a business trip—the business of Drug smuggling. This old Craftsman-style home would probably be worth something but Cisco let the upkeep slide just enough to render it inconspicuous.

Now it's more of a cross between a crash pad for his gang member buddies and a one-stop-shop for hypes and junkies. The gang slangs heroin mostly but they're smart enough to keep things on the down-low so the neighbors don't complain and the police don't get into the habit of visiting.

Cisco leads the notorious El Diablo set of La Faccion' street gang—LF12 for short. They are smaller than most gangs but they enjoy a vicious rep and nobody with half a brain in his head would dare cross them. Cisco, a burly, mustachioed vato in his early forties, enters to the sight of his disheveled mess of a living room. He winces at the deafening music blasting from the stereo. Cisco happens to hate Tejano Mariachi music, especially when it's blaring.

Cisco can be described as a Criminal truest. It's all he can do to control his temper as he walks past people lounging in his home. They instinctively jump to attention. He enters the kitchen to find, Joker a grizzled career-criminal-type, playing poker with his fellow Choloes.

"What is this?" Cisco barks. Aware of his reputation, the men freeze.

"Oh, Cisco... Hey, Man, me and the homies was just kind of kicking back," Joker explains.

"Oh, I get it. So, I'm out here handling business and you're kicking back?"

"Naw, Cisco... it ain't like that. We was waiting to hear back from you man, that's all." Joker also happens to be Cisco's cousin, which is the only reason he tolerates the slob of a man at all. Cisco made him second in command of El Diablo and daily reconsiders his decision.

Cisco grabs Joker by his collar and pulls him in closer. "Joker, you're slipping, Homes. Get your head in the game Vato or I swear on my kids..."

"Yeah, yeah, man, of course... my bad," Joker simpers. He wipes the table clean of cards and attempts to pocket the money but is stopped just short. Cisco relieves him of his winnings as tribute.

"So, everything went down cool then, no witnesses?" Cisco verifies.

"Nope! Nobody saw nothing."

Cisco eyes suspiciously. "Show me."

The men upend their card table to reveal a hidden door leading down to the basement. Joker leads the way as Cisco drifts along behind him.

Inside the underground tavern, is dark, wet, and smelly—the perfect conditions for a hostage. Cisco and Joker watch Mao Lei, through security cameras placed in her small cell. She is curled into a bundle of herself, and bathed in infra-red light.

"She can't see a thing, Man," Joker assures. "But we got night vision cameras fixed on her."

The terrified and sobbing Mao Lei gropes around, helplessly in the dark. Her high-pitched wails would grate on Cisco's nerves but this tomb is soundproof so no one outside of her cell will ever be the wiser.

"So, what are we supposed to do with her?"

"Nothing, yet."

"So, we just gonna babysit her ass?" Joker chuckles.

"Hey, does it really matter? When you get 150 bands for a quick job like this, you don't ask questions," explains Cisco.

"I'm just saying I don't trust this guy," Joker persists. "What if he's just tryin' to set us up against the Asians?"

"It's more like the other way 'round, Esse," Cisco replies. "The way I got it figured… pretty soon the Chinks and the Waps are gonna waste each other anyway. So, we just chill, and when the time is right, we stomp out what's left!"

"This General guy, he musta been pretty impressed with you, huh?" Joker slaps Cisco on the shoulder and quickly realizes his error when his touch-sensitive cousin looks at his misplaced hand. Joker quickly removes it.

For the next two weeks, our city is treated to an almost daily, explosion of gang violence. The death toll escalates to wartime numbers, with bodies turning up everywhere as innocent citizens hide away in their homes from pure terror.

Police Commissioner David Hurst assembles a special Task Force, codenamed 'Scorpion' to deal with the problem. An initiative comprised of elite crime fighters and led by Detective Arturo Carone. All the news outlets are a-buzz with Hurst's choice. Arturo is a streetwise, mild-mannered, and calculated leader. Some assert that unbridled ambition is his prime motivator and he does not deny it. A product of San Francisco's inner-city school system, Arturo decided at a young age that he would dedicate his life to chipping away at the grimy crime-ridden under-belly of San Francisco until he reached the gooey law-abiding center of hippy peace and love that he was sure still lie underneath.

By this time Arturo has already made great progress in keeping the smaller criminal elements in check and although the public loves him for it—the city's new urban-battlefield trend is definitely a personal setback.

Arturo surprises everyone by choosing Detective Sonny Bates as his Scorpion second in command, but he is a firm believer in the energetic, out-of-the-box thinking the youthful officer brings to the table. Sonny, at thirty-one years old, is a brash, smart-mouthed second-year Narco officer. The latest in a long line of flat-foots, he never saw a fight he wanted to back away from. His often-erratic Cowboy antics keep Arturo on his toes, literally.

The officers are called to an early morning homicide on a Sunday. Four Mobster types have been gunned down in a car at the back of a downtown ally. Officer Byron Johnson, a Mid-twenties cadet with donut and coffee connoisseur looks, was the first to arrive on the scene and stands guard.

"Hey, Johnson, how's it going?" Arturo greets.

"Shit, man, gotta pick up extra shifts to pay for this damn vacation my wife wants to go on... Colorado! I keep telling her ass, black people don't ski!" he grumbles.

Sonny cannot resist the opportunity to jab his associate. "You should have told her fat people don't ski," he advises.

Hey man, I keep telling you my wife ain't that big!" Officer Johnson insists.

"I'm talking about your, unhealthy built ass." Sonny pokes Officer Johnson's belly.

Arturo looks closely at the victims—familiar faces, all. He grimaces with realization. "Sonny, take a look at this."

Sonny breaks away from shooting the shit to look over the bullet-riddled corpses. "Whoa, is that who I think it is?" he asks, his eyes gleaming with more excitement than concern. In his mind, the stakes of this drug war have just been raised.

"Yep, Marco Diamante, the Don's stepson. There's going to be hell to pay when The Family finds out about this." Arturo's expression hardens as his brain manufactures scenes of bloodshed and innocent lives lost.

Sonny notices something on the dashboard. It's a rare water lily—an obvious message from Nu Dinh. "So, this is a Yukoshi hit then, right?"

"Yeah, looks that way."

Where am I during this episode? In a bad mood, thanks to an hour spent fighting traffic on my way to SFO. Waiting at the bottom of an arrival escalator reminds me of one of those international dating shows. The excitement amidst other eager receivers is contagious and I begin to get happy feet. Not to mention the knot of anticipation I feel growing inside me, tightening every muscle and causing me to crush the edges of the 'Welcome Home' sign I've made for Candace—a visual masterpiece of Magic Marker, glue, and leftover Stripper glitter.

Just then, I spot her. Candace, my bi-racial beauty bestie—who looks like Jessica Alba's younger prettier sister; if she had one. She is short and slim—a perfectly proportioned dancer statue. "Biiiiiissch!" I scream, overflowing with emotion.

"Hey Biiiissch!" she screams back. We embrace as tightly as the day we were separated. Now let's be clear, this is the only Bitch I don't mind calling me a Bitch, cuz this is my Mutha fuckin Bitch!!!

"Oh my God, look at you!" I demand.

"Check it," she coos, modeling her kick-ass framework for me. She is a pure Diva so the people around me also have no choice but to stop and pay homage.

"Damn, I've missed you! Where are your bags?"

Candace tugs at the strap of her bulky purse. "This is it, I shipped everything else," she says.

"Shipped?"

"Jea this isn't just a vacation. Your girl is officially back... for good!"

I absorb the news with delight, shock, and possibly a little apprehension. She is amused by my dropped jaw. I blink hard and hug her again. "Well shit, then... let's get to gettin'!" I throw my arm around her and guide her out of the terminal.

The drive towards home is a campfire moment filled with amazing stories of Broadway performances, intense auditions, celebrity social gatherings, and sex-capades that boggle my woefully Man-anemic mind. I can barely concentrate on the road as we trip all over our words, unable to get them out fast enough in our exhilaration. To my relief, it's like we've never been apart.

"Then he gone try and tell me... it's nothing to trip out about cuz that's just the way it goes in the music bizz; like that makes the shit okay or something!" she completes the story of one such encounter.

"Wow, are you shitting me?" is all I know to say, not having any recent or relatable conquests to draw from, it seems appropriate.

"I swear I wanted to slap him dead in his stupid face! Oow, I hate him!" she admits. "Sooooo, what about you, Chicka... screwing anyone special?"

Damn it, I've been listening so intently that I forgot to make up a story of my own. But this is Candace... do I really want to lie to her, again?

"Girl please, these dudes out here are total lames. I ain't even trying to play myself like that," I declare, to Candace's delight. Ever the Social Butterfly, she never allowed me to bring sand to the beach. One year she even convinced me to break up with a guy for the weekend so we would be free to mingle in CABO without moral restriction.

"Well good, cuz we are two of the hottest hunnies in Frisco and we're gonna tear this city **_down_**, tonight!" Candace alerts.

Laughing at my girl, like old times completely invigorates me and I'm ready for anything. We stop at a red light and, I notice Candace eyeing me deviously.

"What?" I demand.

"You know what. Red light, Biiiisch," Candace grins like the cute little Devil on my shoulder I protest, "Oh my God, you're playing, right?"

Candace turns up the radio, jumps out of the car, and begins to dance in the street. Yeah, I join her, but in my defense; it's another crossroads moment.

Mayne, you should have seen all those thirsty guys in surrounding cars begin to cheer and whistle. Even the knuckle-head D-bags riding in cars with chicks try, unsuccessfully, to look away.

The street workers are mesmerized by our bodies rocking. A man waiting near us stares and bobs his head to the beat—his girl doesn't appreciate his participation so much. She smacks the back of his head.

A quick glance at my watch tells me, "Shoot we're going to be late."

We quickly dash back into my car and blaze through the yellow light leaving the on-lookers stuck on red once again. We laugh hysterically.

Oh my God, I haven't done anything like that in so long, Candace admits and I have to agree. Life just hasn't been nearly as fun since my CandaNce left.

"So, what now?" she inquires.

I smile deviously.

CHAPTER 7

CITY UNDER SIEGE

While Candace and I select our best 'come-get-me' outfits for the evening, the Scorpion team joins the ongoing shoot-out between the Yukoshi and Mob families which happens to be taking place on one of the busiest streets in the city. Dozens of pedestrians are caught in the crossfire as they run screaming for their lives. A few innocents have already been mowed down during the gun show. Several news vans also get in the way, adding to the chaos. These are violent, desperate men who have decided the only way to survive this mess will be by fighting their way out.

Detectives Carone and Bates arrive Mid-Cluster-fuck and attempt to get control of the situation before it gets any more out of hand. They dive for cover behind a parked squad car where a young lineman cadet, Officer Jason Leander, has already taken shelter.

"Alright, talk to me," Arturo instructs.

"Sir, we got at least twenty unidentified gunmen, we suspect belong to the Yukoshi and fifteen or so combatants. Witnesses say several men dressed in black suits entered the Ming Dragon restaurant a little after 0:1500 hours and opened fire on the customers."

"Civilian casualties?"

"Tons... and we can't get close enough to see if there're any hostages. The other guys have been made as probable Mafia resources. They're dug in pretty deep, and it doesn't look like they want to surrender."

"Never a dull moment," proclaims Sonny.

Arturo thinks for a moment. "Alright, tell your men to lay down some cover fire."

While the officer relays his order, Arturo confers with Sonny. "I need you to run interference!" Arturo unlocks the safety on his gun.

"You got it... but what are you gonna do?"

Arturo surveys the area, seeking a good vantage point. "I'm going to even the odds."

The partners split. Arturo dashes into an alley-way between the restaurant and another building. Sonny appropriates an armored van.

Arturo jumps onto the top of a dumpster, then uses a fire escape ladder to scale the adjoining building. Once he reaches the roof, the Detective discovers, to his frustration, that he still has to make a jump over a wide gap to get to the restaurant rooftop. He backs up as far as he can and sprints toward the building, diving across the gap and narrowly clearing the ledge. As the Detective dives across the gap; his side-arm plummets from its holster to the ground below. Furious, he uses the adrenaline surge to drive him forward.

Several Yukoshi members are on the roof—their backs to Arturo, shooting at his men in the street below. The veteran cop creeps towards them.

Back at ground level, Sonny revs the van's engine. He speeds toward the restaurant as gangsters pump led into the truck. Fortunately, that does little more than scratch its bulletproof sides. Sonny smashes through the barricade of vehicles the shooters are hiding behind. Other Scorpion officers rush in, guns blazing, and subdue the mobsters. They attempt to enter the restaurant but loyal Yukoshi soldiers engage them in heavy gunfire.

On the roof, a Yukoshi enforcer, Namon Tre, barks commands at the other troops. He turns and walks toward the rooftop staircase entrance, where Arturo is waiting—hidden. The Detective grabs Namon's gun and uses him as a shield, demoting Tre's men into spurting blood sacks in a hail of fire. Arturo wastes no time making his way down to the restaurant, slaughtering Yukoshi members at every level. He creeps towards Dao Lam, another fish-faced Yukoshi assassin, and Dinh relative, for a sneak attack. Before our hero can get the drop on the unsuspecting criminal, he's caught off guard and winged by another combatant.

The Detective winces as the bullet cuts through his shoulder. The henchman seizes the moment and begins to unleash marshal punishment upon the sneaky Detective. The two men struggle and soon Dao joins in. Both men get their digs in on Arturo's mug—but just as they are about to end him, Sonny makes a surprise appearance. He is able to change the odds with one well-aimed headshot.

Dao Lam and several Yukoshi fighters, bolt.

Later, as Sonny performs an impromptu birds-eye examination of his partner's wound at the crime scene, I am deciding whether or not to wear my tan Jimmy Chews for tonight's outing and expending just as much concentration. Candace and I have decided on going to Club Beamers because she knows the owner and he's promised her a VIP table with bottle service. She always scores these types of perks as a result of her random, pretty-girl-hook-ups. As her best friend I'm an indirect beneficiary.

The line of people waiting to enter is bursting by the time we arrive, but we stroll right passed those losers to the VIP entrance. Their hateful expressions are worth a thousand Bitch-slaps and I can't help but revel in it. The club is crowded to overflowing with all the right kinds of people, or at least that's what my little friend tells me to ease my nerves.

Beamer's is one of those dark places presided over by a popular DJ who cranks out an endless supply of tuneage. I can tell that it was originally meant to be heterogeneous, by the artfully arranged mismatched vintage 80's furniture that lines the sides of the dance floor to help give it an Art Nouveau 'European Salon' kinda vibe. A blue, star-patterned neon ceiling provides the only light. Striking cocktail waitresses, dressed in white satin skirt-tuxes, parade around with drinks.

The owner, Terry-something, has two giant bouncers usher us behind velvet ropes to the best table in the club, where a bottle of Black label spirits awaits us. And although I'd love to get 'socially acceptable wasted' the dance floor is calling my name.

Candace, however, has downed three shots before I can blink. The bass-instilled music hits my spirit almost immediately. I jiggle in my chair, alerting Candace to the Mexican-Jumping-Beans in my shoes and she accepts my invite. I can't contain my grin.

Candace gazes like a stalking lioness at the herd of eligible young men strutting their stuff on the glowing hardwood floor. Before I know it, I'm approached by a handsome bear of a man. He smiles, charmed by my willingness to be led as he whisks me around the room.

I glance to my right and see Candace in the arms of a young man dressed in a vest and bow tie. That's always been her type—the prim, scholarly pretty boys who straddle the fence just between clean-cut and closeted. I never understood it; they're not my type at all.

After we've worked up a proper lather, the kind that mixes well with perfume and drives dudes to sniffing like rodents, Candace and I head for the bar.

Antonio Abraynas, an attractive, wavy-haired young Puerto Rican Papi, watches us from further down the bar before he finally gathers the courage to come over and speak.

"Hey don't I know you?" he suggests.

"No... I don't think so," I reply.

"Oh, okay… well sorry, I'm Antonio, nice to meet you." He offers his hand, and graciously I shake it."

"Hi, I'm Jeadda and this is Candace." I present the little hot-rod beside me. Candace waves dismissively while checking her messages.

"Well, would you ladies like something to drink… I'm buying,"

"No, thank you… we're fine.

Candance is fed up with the niceties. "You gotta be kidding me… is that your spill? Uh duh um do I know you, you look so familiar. No, well let me buy you a drink blah blah blah…That was corny dude… Promise me you'll never do that again, in life!" I take it the drinks have kicked in.

The man eyes me oddly but before I can speak his face flashes a really peculiar expression of revelation, "Wait… Eye Candy… You're Starr right?"

Oh, shit… Busted again! I quickly snatch up Candace and drag her, through the crowd, towards the exit. Antonio tries to follow but he's not as experienced at dodging drunks. "Ladies! Come back! Was it something I said?" The look on his face is priceless, but that was a close call and I know I won't be able to hold on to this secret much longer.

While I am trying to escape a barrage of Candace's 'WTF' questions on the drive home, Arturo sits on a gurney at the county hospital. Cold, sterile, cloroxy smells chew their brains as Arturo gets stitched up by a skinny effeminate male nurse. Sonny hovers around the nurse—concerned.

"I know you must've used up at least eight of your nine lives by now, old man. It's a good thing you have me around to protect you," Sonny jokes to calm himself—perhaps his partner too.

"Hey, Imma go get some coffee—you want a donut or something?"

Arturo grins. "Yeah, sure."

"No problem… Batman."

"Robin." The men bump fists and Sonny trots off on his errand.

A needle pierces Arturo's skin and he flinches in pain. "Oww... Really?"

The Nurse cleans Arturo's wound once more. "Alright, there you go. You'll just want to keep it clean and dry," he says. "So... how long have you two been together" he infers.

"Sometimes it feels like years," Arturo smirks, oblivious to the context of his nurse's intrusion.

"You're so cute together," the nurse gushes. Arturo's face is suddenly identical to the Riddler's boxers—see that was a Batman reference too? Oh whatever, if a guy had said that shit, ya'll woulda been all hoots and hollers.

Suddenly, Captain Carswell, sticks his blocky buzz-cut head through the curtain in search of his two hero cops.

"Hey, Cap," Arturo acknowledges.

"Arturo... you okay?" Carswell inquires.

"Yeah, I'll survive," Arturo assures his Commander.

"Where's your more annoying half?"

"Sonny's in the Caffe. Did we find out anything else about the hit?" Arturo gingerly slides back into his shirt.

"We were able to confirm this was a hit by The Family—big surprise there. They're targeting Yukoshi businesses in retaliation for Marco Diamante's murder." Carswell sighs at the subsequent bad news. "The Commissioner is bringing in FBI and ATF to assist with the operation," he reports.

"What... are you kidding me, Captain? Sonny and I have been building this case for months now... We've lost good men! I'm not just going to hand my team's lives over for some bureaucratic...!"

The Captain interrupts hissing, "Hey, hey... I'm not saying 'take over', Arthur; just assist." He always calls Arturo—Arthur for some reason. I wonder if he even knows that's not his real name. I wonder if Arturo ever bothered to correct him.

"Danny, I promise you... if you just give us a little more time, I know we can get..."

"Look, let's face it... we're in over our heads here, Arthur. We're losing this battle, son. Whether you like it or not, we need help."

At that moment, Sonny returns with a donut and coffee. "Here ya go, brother. Sonny's brand of special medicine." Sonny notices Carswell. "Hey Cap'n... what'd I miss?"

"Honey, your lover's honor is at stake. You'd better drop that donut and defend his finely sculpted self," the nurse exclaims.

Sonny and Arturo glance at the Nurse, then at each other. Finally, a look of understanding slaps them in the face, and they quickly back away from one another.

Arturo increases the bass in his voice and reports, "The Commissioner in his infinite wisdom is trying to bring in the Feds on our case."

"You shittin' me, right? Captain... tell me he's joking?" Sonny implores.

"Look him, I can listen to gripe; you my friend are another story, entirely," Carswell reminds the fledgling detective. "Arthur, you need to get on board with this. Don't make me sideline you."

Meanwhile, somewhere, the villain known as Dunlock; watches news coverage of the day's gunfight. Blakk sits near him. "Do you see this? How easily fooled they are? Our enemies are emotional and weak, like women," asserts Dunlock.

Dunlock reaches over to a fish tank and breaks a water lily off at the stem. He examines it and repeats: "Fools."

Candace and I return to my place after a late-night raid of 'Jack in the Crack,' to get her something that'll help counteract the alcohol.

I drag her inebriated ass back into my place and sit her down in my father's reading chair—the only memento of his I was able to retain.

"Oh, what was his name again... Michael, Michael?" she mumbles in Drunk-Girl-Speech.

"... Mike Creasy," I assist.

"Yeah... oow girl, Greasy Creasey, with that damn S-curl. Oh my God, and it smelled too! I can't believe I let him take me to Homecoming!"

Another fascinating character trait of my friend is her penchant for drunk-truth-telling episodes that she never remembers once she sobers up.

"Well, you always loved them, bright-skinned dudes," I remind her.

"Girl, that Nigga told me he was part Puerto Rican!"

"Wasn't he?" I know the answer but I need to keep her awake while I pull out the sofa bed or I'll have to carry her ass, again.

"Hell's no; that Nigga ain't even Meskan! His parents were black as hell! That bastard let me introduce myself to his Momma in Spanish too! Bitch looked at me like I was half crazy!"

I laugh at the thought. "At least you didn't give him any," I commend her.

I am greeted by silence. I turn around to find Candace, looking guilty as sin.

"Eww, you 'Hoe bag! You let him...?"

"No girl, of course not," she stammers. "I just let him finger me." In Candace's mind that isn't sexual intercourse and therefore not as bad.

"You slut... what about our pact? Not until college, remember?" I laugh at the naive freshman pact made between separated sisters. That was one commitment I had kept despite the hordes of Hormone crazed teen-aged boys trying to get my goodies.

"I know, Girl, but he just kept begging and wouldn't shut the hell up unless..."

"Unless you let him paw your cooch?" I ask. "Whatever. Anyway, here you go. It ain't the Hilton but it's soft."

Too late—Candace has already curled up into a tight little human-sized knot on the chair. As I cover her with a blanket, I'm reminded of the broken little girl who had just lost her father, clinging to me for comfort. I vowed then to protect her from hurt at any cost. Who knew that promise would turn into an eight-year lie? Some best friend I am.

By the next evening, I've made enough excuses to Candace about my night job for her not to follow me, all while conveniently neglecting to tell her what it is I do. At Club Eye Candy, I finish my set, on Stage one and can't help but realize how deliberately I'm moving looking forward to my release. I become so fixated on the clock I fail to see a particular group of men making their way into the club.

Blakk, Reese, and several T.R.A.P. henchmen are met by a suspicious, Sir Mont'e. "Good evening gents… welcome to Club Eye Candy," he greets.

"This your club?" Blakk inquires. "Impressive—for a strip joint."

Sir Mont'e is nonplussed. "What can I get for you, Pimpin?"

"It's been a long week. Make sure my associates have a good time." Blakk hands Sir a wad of money and pats him on the head like a child. Sir's quick, Chi-town-forged temper flares at being handled in such a way.

"What the… did this Mutha…?" Then he realizes how much money he's just been handed. Let's just say it's enough to warrant overlooking a head pat.

"You were saying?" Blakk asks.

"Umm, nothing. Brotha, don't you worry about a thing. My ladies will make sure your boys're well taken care of, or my name isn't Ben Franklin, Franklin… Franklin," a preoccupied Sir chants as he counts big-face bills.

Sir Mont'e steps behind the bar and gets on the intercom. "Uh, all freaks, to the VIP lounge for a Code Green. I repeat, a Code Green in VIP. Ladies come get this money immediately!"

A stampede of, 'Go Getters' streams up the stairs into the Main Room. Go-Getters are what we call those Professional Negotiators—the ladies who can squeeze the last dollar out of a broken vending machine. They mob the VIP room like Hornets. As always, proper Stripper Etiquette prevails. No more than two girls to a trick unless otherwise requested—it keeps things from getting too catty.

Personally, I'm glad my shift is over. On my way to the dressing room, I'm nearly run over by Monica. Hah! She must have heard the dinner bell late. "Hey Starr, where you going?" she asks. "Didn't you hear? There's Ballers in VIP. It's a Code Green, Girl!" she informs.

"Naw girl, I'm going home. My shift just ended. But you go get your money, Sis."

"You know it!" she exclaims. Such a sweet kid; that youthful exuberance should take her far. Can't say I've ever been that way about working here, but as I've said there are some moments, I'm on stage, that I can block out all of the smoke and catcalls to reach my zone inside a song.

The dressing room is quiet except for the distant hollow thud of bass pumping through the walls. Usually, I relish a break from the stripper-small-talk, but tonight I'm consumed by my recollection of Cofaxx's proposal. Wondering why he had chosen me? Was it simply my familiarity with our mutual enemy? Or had he seen something in me? Something Bad Ass! Can I really help take down a Drug King Pin? The very idea seems so ludicrous, but the memory of my parent's execution makes it very appealing.

Passing his empty office, I decide that Sir must've placed the employee exit where it is, so he'd have a direct bead on anyone sneaking out. His sudden appearance blocking my path confirms my suspicions. "Starr, I need you in VIP," he insists. "Your little hot ass friend disappeared and I'm one short. I swear, I'm trying to run a God damn business here, and ya'll insubordinate asses is messing with my overhead!"

I remind him that my shift has ended. He reminds me that any veteran would know better than to leave with that kind of dough being flashed around. But even at the risk of Sir's mighty-mouse-wrath, there is absolutely no way I'm dancing another step on these aching feet. "Sorry, Sir, but my shift is over. Plus, I feel my cycle coming on," I whine.

The nauseous look on Sir's face as he cuts me off, tells me I've succeeded. "Ugh, say less. Get outta here and take your Aunt Flo with you. I'll see you in three days." I'm not sure how creeped out I should be that he knows how long my cycle lasts, but either way, I don't wait for a second opinion.

"Thank you, Sir." I plant a soft kiss of appreciation on his cheek and continue on my way. I stop to thank Keith again for his attempt to defend me. The Doctor says he's going to have to wear that arm brace for six more weeks and although I feel terrible, I dare not tell him about my subsequent encounter with Cofaxx.

Suddenly, a bone-chillingly, familiar smell drifts passed me: Leather and cheap booze. Cofaxx's offer has obviously got me spooked, I tell myself, on my way out the door; completely oblivious that I so narrowly avoided bumping into Blakk.

CHAPTER 8

UNCOMFORTABLE TRUTHS

It's Midday somewhere along Al Meda Boulevard. Frederico Menza, a twenty-year-old, wiry Hispanic hustler, emerges from a liquor store carrying a pack of skittles and an iced-tea drink. He ogles a cute girl at the corner.

"Damn Baby, you sexy... what's your name?"

"I gotta man," she responds, impervious to his charm.

"Great, but that's not what I asked you," he insists.

The lady doesn't break stride crossing the street. "That's okay, I bet he can't beat it like me!" he continues. Too late—she's gone.

Arturo and Sonny screech to a stop at the curb. Freddy recognizes them immediately and his irritation is evident. The buddy cops, jump out of the car and approach him. Freddy has been one of their citizen informants for years.

"Freeeeeddy, what's up, you big ol' Pimp, you," Sonny greets him sarcastically.

Freddy grimaces. "Damn, why ya'll always coming down here messing with me, son?"

Like most CIs, Freddy's involvement with the Detectives is not exactly voluntary. Fred's not too bright, but luckily for him he's blessed with a motor mouth and a photographic memory.

"Shut up, Stupid... and stop talking like that, you're from Ohio," Sonny warns. Needless to say, he and Freddy aren't what you might call, Chummy.

"Come on Fredrick, you know what this is... get up against the fence," Arturo commands. Detective Bates pushes him roughly against a chain-link fence.

"Damn, man, watch it, yo!" Freddy protests.

"So, Fred... you been keeping your ear to the streets, right? I need some info," Arturo alerts.

"Naw man, I been sick with the flu." Freddy coughs in Sonny's direction and earns another shove against the gate for it.

"Oh, so you want to do this the hard way? Alright, let's go; get in the car," Arturo commands.

"I can't. I got some clothes over at the Laundromat..."

"Hey, get your ass in this car, before I <u>PUT</u> you in the car!" Sonny threatens.

Without waiting for a response, he cuffs Freddy and hustles him into the back seat. "Might as well make this look official," he whispers in the CI's ear. Freddy's an asshole but neither detective wants to get him killed.

As they drive off. "Yo man, these cuffs are too tight, B. You fools is violating my rights," Freddy whines.

"Hey, I'm about to reach back there and violate your face!" Sonny asserts.

"Alright, Son... chill!" Freddy suggests. "You need to switch to decaf, B."

Arturo snaps his fingers. "Freddy... pay attention. What do you know about this war between The Mobsters and the Yukoshi?"

Freddy dips into his memory to scoop out a spoonful of intel. "Well, people are saying, the Don took something the China-men want and now Nu Dinh's vowed to destroy everything the Italians have built until he gets it back," Freddy reports.

"Well, what'd they take?" Sonny probes.

"That's just it, nobody knows. Whatever it is, it's more valuable to Dinh than anything."

"What are the homeboys doing about this?" Arturo inquires.

"Shiiit... not a damn thing. Vatos don't want 'nothing to do with that shit!" Freddy says. "Aye yo, hold up, how much am I getting for this info, anyway?"

"Man, you haven't even given us anything we don't already know!" Sonny snorts. He is usually the Bad Cop to Arturo's Good Cop in these situations. Arturo pulls to a stop in a vacant lot.

"Oh yeah, well I bet you didn't know, LF12 has a huge heroin plant on the Northside." Freddy can't help it—he leaks like a facet– divulging this news before he's negotiated his fee.

"Where?" Arturo asks.

"That depends. What's it worth to you, B?" Freddy grins, triumphantly.

"Boy, Imma smack that fake ass accent!" Sonny lunges at Freddy but he's collared by the Good Cop.

"Sonny... relax," Arturo instructs. He hands Freddy a one-hundred-dollar bill.

Freddy accepts the generous donation. "See? That's how you conduct business," he tells Bates.

"Hey... Address, Wise-ass?" Arturo insists—his time is running out and his patience, wearing thin.

"It's over on Old Railway Street, in this warehouse. Won't do you much good though. You know they got that place locked down tighter than Fort Knox." He holds the money up to the light. "This ain't counterfeit, is it?"

"Goodbye, Fred."

Sonny exits to uncuff their detainee in an isolated area. "What the hell you mean, B? I don't even know where we at!" Freddy argues while exiting the car, anyway. He knows better than to protest too much.

"Use your brain, Fred. We can't just drop you off back in the hood. You want all the Homies to know you're selling secrets? You won't last a week," Sonny reasons while removing the shackles. He gives Freddy one last push in the head before hopping back into the car.

Freddy flips Sonny the middle finger as the officers drive off. He scratches his head curiously, unable to determine where he is.

The next afternoon finds Candace and me standing in the middle of a cemetery—manicured lawns and willow trees as far as the eye can see. Mausoleums and seven-foot walls block out the living and muffle the city noise. We stare at side-by-side burial plots—my parents, inseparable in life and death. Nearby, Candace's father waits patiently for the love of his life as well.

Why so close? It's silly—I know, but who could deny the request of two grieving kids. Someday, Candace and I will be laid to rest here, too. Poor Candace, even now, visiting that cemetery, it's as if her dad has just been stolen from her all over again. Revealing the true circumstances behind his death will be crippling, but I can't keep this from her any longer and call myself her true friend.

Our traditional, post-graveside lunch at Sasha's Soul Food has done a lot to console us over the years. There's nothing like smothered pork chops, mashed potatoes, and collard greens to really put the tragedies of life into perspective. But today is different—too many long-kept secrets have robbed even me of my appetite and I know there's only one way to escape this torment.

I stir my potatoes while contemplating how best to break the news. Maybe I should wait—take her out for drinks. Alcohol would certainly slow her down if nothing else. Maybe I should have set things straight at the cemetery where there was nothing to pick up and throw at me but a flower bouquet. 'Stop stalling, Jea,' I berate myself.

"Girl, what's wrong with you? You haven't said a word since we left the cemetery," Candace remarks.

"I have something to tell you," I admit.

And I did...

The drive home after my confession isn't as cathartic as I hoped it would be—probably because I didn't expect to be alone with my thoughts. I don't blame Candace for walking out on me. Truthfully, I anticipated much worse. The details of what I said blur in my mind now, but I do remember a lot of rambling pleas for forgiveness. The tears welled up in Candace's eyes and in my heart, I begged them not to fall—no such luck.

"How could you keep this from me?" she raged. "I thought you were my friend!"

I had no answer for her. I just sat there with my lips parted, waiting for my brain to catch up. She stormed out of the diner and snagged a cab.

My apartment has never felt as empty as it does right now. My only refuge comes in the form of my I-pod and my set of oversized headphones. I drown myself in the most soulful playlist I have.

I allow my mind to drift and who should pop into it but Cofaxx. I imagine him across town, alone in his girly house. He sits in a comfortable chair, sipping a stiff drink and staring at a framed portrait of the wife he lost. He wasn't willing to discuss how it happened, but from the pictures of her during pregnancy, his lack of children, and all the sappy tear-jerker movies I've ever seen, I assume she died tragically. Maybe she went during childbirth. Or maybe she ended up in a horrific traffic accident before she ever even had a chance to give birth. Whatever it was, it had obviously shaken the poor man to his core.

Dunlock, however, was a different subject, entirely. Cofaxx went into great detail about his older brother Di Tiaay Asensea. He told me how, as children, they witnessed the murder of their parents at the hands of rebel militants. How, while his father lay dying, he made Dunlock promise to protect him.

The orphaned boys would steal food from the UNITA camp during the night and the troops were never the wiser. I couldn't imagine two children fooling an army of trained killers but there was an unwavering truth in his eyes that convinced me.

One night after weeks of scavenging undetected, they were finally caught. Dunlock allowed himself to be captured so that Cofaxx could escape. The next day, when the small child returned to look for his brother, he discovered the rebels had packed up camp and fled with Dunlock.

To the best of his ability, the small boy followed the Militants but his body eventually gave way to the elements. A Missionary Group of students saved Cofaxx from severe dehydration and he was taken to their Mission to recover. Cofaxx was relocated to Europe and then to the American foster care system because his mother had been an American citizen. Once he came of age, he was able to leave his group home and join a new family—the US Marine Corps, in Pensacola Florida. By that time, he had married a young elementary school teacher named Lauren. He abruptly ended his story as he drew closer to an explanation of her untimely death but I can tell he loves her still.

Dunlock, like many other third-world orphans, was forced into a slave-soldier's life of violence and crime that would ultimately consume him. How could anyone remain sane after being forced to fight, steal and slaughter innocent people? Dunlock eventually grew to embrace the rebel lifestyle, but the regulated structure of UNITA couldn't contain him. His arrogance and love of bloodshed led him to establish his criminal network—T.R.A.P. (The Republic for Angolan Prosperity)

CHAPTER 9

XXX-POSED

It's a bright and unseasonably warm day at Carson Park. Two children, Rebecca and Kaylen something, are playing soccer near a gully when they make a grisly discovery. Rebecca watches as Kaylen lifts a tattered, bloody sheet with a stick. Underneath is the slashed corpse of my young stripper mentee—Monica.

Arturo and Sonny quickly reach the scene. and find the body. Monica hasn't been moved and Forensic specialists are beginning to scout the area for evidence. "So, what are we looking at?" Arturo asks one of them.

"Deceased female; early twenties. Beaten and strangled—No ID, no clothes. A couple of footprints. Some kids found the body," one of the specialists reports.

Arturo crouches down and lifts the sheet with the tip of a pen. He studies the victim's face, disturbed by what he sees. "Just a baby... is that all?" he asks.

"Too soon to know."

"Alright, get me a full workup on the victim and those tracks."

Arturo and Sonny back off, so the forensics team can do their job. Arturo has another gruesome memory to add to the collection in his head. For him, it's not a mystery: Bad people do bad things.

At this point, I am still unaware that Monica has disappeared. Candace had gone back to her old house after leaving me at the restaurant. Don't worry they still own it. I can't imagine how creepy it must have been in that huge place all alone. Well, to know Candace, is to know a Princess—and nothing cheers up a Princess like a little pampering. I sent her a gift certificate for an expensive Spa Day as my way of saying: 'I'm so sorry.'

By the time the Mani-Pedi-Waxi-Spa-Day is done, my friend has cooled off. So of course, outside the spa, she is handed a flyer promoting Club Eye Candy. And guess whose sticky buns are plastered all over it... Mine! Busted yet again! I guess we're all truly working with the cards life deals us.

Naturally, I can't decide how to react when Candace enters the club. I grasp at straws: 'Finally, this will be a chance to clear the air.' Candace lingers near the door, surveying the room. I instinctively seek out Sir. 'Damn it, he's already headed straight for her!'

Sir swoops in like a ghetto pigeon and kisses Candace's hand. "Well, hello, Sunshine, may I help you?"

"Oh, hi there... Umm?" Candace waits for Sir to introduce himself.

"Sir," he replies.

She looks at him, curiously. "Sir...?"

"Sir Mont'e. I'm the owner of this fine establishment," he boasts.

"So, your name is 'Sir'?"

"Yes Nigga, Sir... it's a word!"

Finally, my song ends and I rush off stage, forgetting my tips. I flash across the club and slide right between them.

"I'm sorry, Sir, this is my friend, Candace. Don't mind her, she was just leaving," I explain. I try to pull Candace away from him but she refuses to budge.

"No, I wasn't leaving!" she insists.

"Yes, you were!" I frown at her—a tactic that used to fold her like a cheap lawn chair, but tonight she gives it right back to me.

"You're not my father, Jeadda. Rumor has it, he was murdered!" I have to admit the comment does its job to shut my damn mouth.

I glance at Sir in time to watch his mouth drop open. He quickly recovers. "Leaving? Aww, Starr, don't be crazy, she just got here. I haven't even had a chance to show her my palace yet." He shews me away and leads Candace by her hand towards the bar. "Would you care for a drink, pretty girl?"

"As a matter of fact, I'd love a drink, Mr. Sir, sir."

"Just Sir will do fine for now." He glances back over his shoulder. "Uhh, Starr, get back to work—chop, chop!" He imperiously claps his hands twice.

As they head for the bar, I can hear him attempting to turn on the old Chi-town charm. "That's just terrible about your father. You know, my daddy died a few years ago too."

"Oh, I'm sorry to hear that, if you don't mind, what happened?"

"My momma happened. Terrible, just terrible! We had a closed casket and everything..."

So, the night's almost over and I haven't seen Candace since she and Sir disappeared from the bar. Can't say I'm too worried, because I know Sir has certain rules. He never has sex with anyone the first time he meets them. It's a weird superstition of his. I imagine he probably got burned once or got tricked by one of those really pretty Trans chicks.

Just as I am about to end my shift, Candace appears near my stage. She pulls out some bills and waves them at me—she must be drunk.

"Woohoo seeeeexy, take it off!"

I gather my tips and exit the stage. She blocks my path. "So, I've been thinking and... you're right. Sir helped me to see that I probably wouldn't have been able to handle knowing my father was murdered, back then. Shit, I was still trying to get up the nerve to wear colored nail polish." She tears up. "So... I guess... thank you for... you know... being there for me."

Much to my surprise and my relief, she throws her arms around me and hugs me tight. And to think I had Sir to thank for setting her straight. I can almost hear the huge weight I've been carrying hit the floor. Then she smiles slyly and I know there's a Big ol' 'But' coming. "Guess what? Sir offered me a job. He even said we could work the same shift. Isn't that great?"

That sneaky Bastard!!! I know my lack of a Poker-face gives my disappointment away but I don't care. "Candace, trust me—you do not want to work here!" I reprimand.

"Why not? You seem to like it," she pouts.

"There are a million places I'd rather be. You're better than this... you've made the big time, why turn back now?"

"I'm sick of New York... I'm sick of scripted chorus lines... and I'm sick of everyone expecting me to be a good little girl! Besides, if you hate it so much, then why do you do it," she grills.

"Maybe because this is the real world and we don't all have a trust fund. This is the only way I can get paid for doing what I love." The words slip out before I can stop them.

"In other words, you're afraid. You've just got all these excuses for why you can't succeed. So, what, if I had a different life? Trust fund or not, at least I'm willing to try. Have you ever even tried or do you just spend your time complaining?"

Ouch! I struggle to explain that it isn't envy for her money or abilities. Nor do I think I deserve it more than her—it's simply the frustration of having a gift and never being given a chance to use it. After all, what else are God's gifts for if not to use them? Even I know that and I'm no Jesus-freak. I don't admit it, but what Candace just said, shakes me.

Candace remains defiant. "Jea look, I'm grateful to you for always having my back," she admits. "But, I'm not a scared little kid anymore and I don't need your permission. I just need you to be my girl. Can't you just be my girl on this one?" Her mind is made up. I have no choice but to concede and accept another hug. I never articulate it, but I feel that, somehow, her dancing alongside me legitimizes my own choice.

A few nights later, the Detectives stop by Jamison's Pub. Its dark paneled walls and heavy leather booths scream: 'Mancave'. Jamison's has been a popular police watering hole since the 1940s. Arturo, the Alpha Male of the team, directs Sonny to get them a pool table, while he buys a round of drinks. He makes his way to the long mahogany bar, where he finds an old friend.

"Hey, Old Man."

The bar's owner, Michael Jamison, comes straight from Irish Central Casting. He leans his thick, hairy arms across the bar to shake the hand of his pal. "Well, what do ya know… Arty my boy, how the hell are yah?"

"How's it going, Mike?"

Mike throws his hands up. "Shit, brother, you know me. Just getting younger and prettier every day. How's about you, haven't seen you around these parts in a forever."

"Yeah man, I'm just showing my partner the old neighborhood." Arturo points to Sonny who has already made himself at home, yucking it up with a few off-duty officers.

"So how you liking it uptown?" Michael asks.

"Well, it's different, I'll say that. The drinks aren't as stiff," Arturo admits.

Michael grins. "You better believe it. Those buttoned-up yuppies don't know how to party. What can I get for you, Brother?"

"Let's go with two whiskeys... oh, and a couple of brews." Michael grabs the bottle of his namesake from a nearby shelf and pours several fingers into two neat glasses.

As he yanks a few ice-cold brews from his cooler, Michael proclaims, "Man, it must be Halloween or something. All the old ghosts are coming out."

The statement catches Arturo's curiosity. With one of the bottles, Michael gestures at another familiar face: Luther Cofaxx, sipping a drink in a corner booth.

Arturo leans in. "Oh wow, is that Luther? Man, I haven't seen him since he quit the force. What's he up to nowadays?"

"Couldn't tell you. Seems neither of you has much time for your old buddy Mike, anymore," Michael clucks.

Moments later, Arturo approaches Cofaxx. "Damn Rookie, you're about as useless as a spare tire on a boat. If I threw you in a lake..."

"... You'd probably die of thirst," Cofaxx completes the quip. He is slightly entertained by seeing his former partner—very slightly. Not that theirs was a contentious relationship, just a part of his past he doesn't care to revisit.

"Wow... It's been a long time, Luther. How you been, partner?"

Cofaxx, ever the cool customer replies, "Well, you know what they say, life is what you make it." He chooses not to go into details and Arturo, remembering how private he is, respects the hint.

"So, I heard you made lead detective," Cofaxx says.

"Yeah man, I'm doing alright. Just showing my new partner the ropes like you did for me." Arturo points out Sonny, who is acting out a bust, and no doubt embellishing the story for the other officers. "Hey, you should join us. I'd like the kid to meet you. That is if you..."

Cofaxx declines the offer without much of an excuse. He rises to his feet and grabs his coat. Before he leaves, Arturo passes him a business card. "If you ever want to hang out or get a drink..."

Cofaxx studies it for a moment. Arturo wonders if he's going to throw it away, but is relieved when the man pockets it. "Well, Detective Carone, you be careful out there." The men shake hands and Luther exits. Arturo makes his way over to Sonny.

"Pretty serious looking guy... who was that?" Sonny asks, accepting the drinks Arturo brought.

"That, was my old partner. He taught me everything I know about being a cop."

"Hmm, that must have been a quick lesson." When Art doesn't respond to his joke, Sonny gently prods him for more information. Arturo sadly recounts the story of Cofaxx's dismissal from the force. Luther Cofaxx was the most decorated officer in their precinct. His devotion to Law and Order might have been his most distinguishing characteristic, if not—for her.

Lauren Carr, was truly Cofaxx's soul mate. Graceful and soft-spoken, she was the Beauty to his Beast. He chased her for months after meeting her at a Commissary exchange shop on his Pensacola, Florida Naval base.

While Cofaxx ascended through the ranks of command, Lauren pursued her Master's in Education at Pensacola State. They married and soon after expected to add a baby boy to their family. Luther decided to leave the Marines after returning from a trip to visit his war-torn homeland. He opted for a career in local law enforcement and the couple settled in San Fran.

Thanks to his exemplary skill and aptitude in training exercises he was quickly promoted. By the time Arturo joined the force, Cofaxx was already a street-tested Sergeant. They were teamed up despite Cofaxx's reluctance to take on a partner.

On a rainy night, about eight months into their partnership, the officers received a call concerning a homicide in the Bernal Heights area.

"Cofaxx drove with the sirens on full blare the whole way and never said a word, but his face was frightening—awash with terror," Arturo recalls.

They pulled up to a home in the Upper-middle-class community and Arturo watched his partner crumble with every step towards the house. Inside lay the only woman Cofaxx had ever loved... Lauren. She'd been bludgeoned and apparently strangled to death in the middle of their living room, still pregnant. Cofaxx fell to his knees and gathered her limp body into his arms. He released an ungodly scream, which still haunts Arturo's memory. Thanks to this one senseless act of violence, he was never the same again.

When his enforced mourning period ended, Luther submerged himself in his work and refused to take even one day off. Obsessed is too weak a word to describe what he became. His erratic and savage pursuit of Lauren's killer prompted the Department to dismiss him as a safety risk.

Arturo takes down a winning shot and eyeballs Sonny. "Both his wife and unborn son... murdered. Can you imagine?"

"Damn, that's messed up," Sonny agrees.

"Horrible." The two Detectives toast Luther Cofaxx in absentia, wishing him well. Then, they re-rack the balls and begin another game.

CHAPTER 10

FRIEND OR FOE

After the heart-to-heart between Candace and me, she heads home and I call Monica again. Finally, I receive an answer but it isn't Monica. "Officer Samuel Gage, who am I speaking with," a commanding voice responds. Before I can speak, a news report about the deceased woman found in the gully flashes at me from the T.V. above the bar.

My knees buckle under me. Although I can't hear the report over the thump of the music; the closed caption message delivers her tragic narrative like a hammer blow. I quickly hang up—sure, I had let my guard down momentarily for Cofaxx, but trust the Boys in blue overnight? They tried to ruin a good man's reputation. So, who knows what they'd try to pin on me?

I naively fight myself to believe that the news reports are some strange mistake—no such luck. They finally go through Sir, summoning me down to make a statement, and Candace volunteers to drive me there. Once there, I am guided into an institutional gray interrogation room where I'm shown pictures of what that Mother-Fucker did to her! The officer questioning me apologizes for insisting I view these photos but says they need any help they can get. If Candace wasn't with me, I would really lose my shit. The cops ask me some of the most asinine questions I've ever heard and it disgusts me. A crime as heinous as this, demands at least some noticeable effort and I'm not seeing it. My heart goes out to Monica's little boy. Who better, than Candace and me to know how this will haunt him for the rest of his life?

Later, we drive up to look-out-point so we can clear our heads. I reflect on Monica and the hopes and dreams she shared with me. Candace listens as I briefly bring her back to life with my account—what a friend. I'm sure she can tell how much that youngin' got to me by the gut-wrenching tone of my voice.

We lean back and watch cheery city lights sparkling off the bay and guzzle Watermelon Vodka. Yeah, I fell off the wagon but it's for Monica, so I've already forgiven myself beforehand. I wonder if by accepting that, this madness as just the way things are—I'm somehow contributing to the notion that such a senseless and brutal act is an inescapable matter of fate.

Candace watches me, anxiously. "Are you gonna be, okay?" she asks.

All I can do is nod.

"It sucks that there are people out there, who devote their lives to preying on the innocent. Somebody should turn the tables on them—see how they like living in fear," she proclaims, before taking another swig.

"You think so, huh?" Little does she know it but Candace has just captured my exact sentiments.

"Hell yeah. If I had the chance to flip the switch on my father's killer, I'd Bar B Que his ass, without hesitation," she rants. Something's certainly different about my little partner in crime, now—she has developed an edge. At that moment, I realize what needs to be done.

"What if there was a way to get payback on the ones who stole our parents from us?"

"Oooow, where do I sign up?" she laughs. "Wait, are you serious?"

I confess I've never been more serious in my life. I'm tired of feeling like a victim—a defenseless nobody, subject to the demented and perverted whims of any psycho with an axe to grind. My fear has become a barricade that keeps me from having a life. It's like somebody opened a flood-gate and all the feelings I've kept bottled up inside tumble out in a waterfall of booze-fueled words. I tell Candace how I daily wake up in a sweat, haunted by my childhood monsters. The night is freezing but I don't care. I get out of the car and throw my fists in the air, shouting at the top of my lungs: "MY DAYS OF LYING DOWN ARE OVER! TODAY IS THE FIRST DAY OF A VICIOUS NEW ME!"

Candace joins me and we jump up and down. I tell her about Luther's offer and together we agree that we want justice, but even more than that, we want revenge!

"Revenge!" For the first time in my life, saying that word fills me with power.

I show up at the address Cofaxx gave me along with Candace and Deseree, a little after noon the next day. Why Deseree? Well, in our excitement about this new adventure, Candace and I got a little too loud in the dressing room, and an eavesdropping Deseree overheard us. She jumped at the idea—if, for no other reason than, to meet Sexy Ninja Bitches. Don't get me wrong, I ain't tryna put anybody in danger, but I don't think I could have stopped her thrill-seeking ass if I tried. Candace and I decide, 'what the hell'—strength in numbers, right?

The building we end up at looks like nothing more than an abandoned warehouse. "You sure this is the place?" Deseree asks, staring at the huge brick fortress.

"Yeah, 500 East Bay Avenue," I say, not wanting to let on that I am secretly just as skeptical.

"Pssh Girl, I think your GPS is broken... this don't look like any gym I've ever been to," she volleys.

"Oh, com'on you guys—how many action movie training montages always take place in buildings just like this," Candace gushes. "It's perfect!"

"Anyway, I never said it was a gym... I said: training facility," I interject. Candace points out how new the double bay entrance doors look—very unusual for a building in this condition.

"So, what are we supposed to do now?" Deseree asks.

I'm not sure. Cofaxx's proposition to me involved joining some team of female crime fighters he called the Sirens. It seemed unbelievable but he said it all serious, like one of those infomercial guys selling Shamwows. He'd personally trained them to take down major criminals. Serious ninja-types that could put a hurting on anyone. I remember joking that Rich and Powerful Crime Lords and Gorgeous Vixens always go hand in hand. He didn't even crack a smile.

Now that I'm here, I can't help but wonder if all this Charlie's Angels shit is just a pipe dream for a guy with a screw loose. Then I remember the huge pile of would-be-rapist he rescued me from. Just then, the bay door begins to open and Cofaxx steps forward to greet us. "Ladies?" he eyes me curiously and my sights catch ground not wanting the smoke. He quickly brushes off my over-step. "Welcome to the HUB. Please, come in," he invites.

We enter cautiously and get our first glimpse of some real James Bond shit. Concealed behind the doors, is a state-of-the-art combat training facility, complete with a gym, weapons, and gadget-loaded vehicles. It's a total vigilante Bat-cave!

Candace and Deseree introduce themselves. Then Cofaxx escorts us through the warehouse. "As you can see, our facility is fully equipped with the latest in combat training and intelligence equipment," Cofaxx declares, with pride. There's a change in him I can't quite mark until I realize... he's happy. It's a grim sort of happiness, but it's there.

At the far end of the cathedral-like building, we see a group of super-fit women engaged in an intense sparring session inside an octagon boxing ring.

Although I try to pay attention to the tour, my eyes are drawn to them. There is Dalia Pierre, code-named Jade, and Ryan Nichols a.k.a. Rayne. I marvel at how well they fight—like men; viciously striking and kicking each other with incredible force. Another chick, Jazmine Lucas or Jazzy, stands inside the ring with them, arbitrating the match.

Apparently, our intrusion does not go unnoticed. Dalia stops and glares at us. Remember that ass-clinching feeling? Well yeah, I'm there right now! I force myself to remember that the new me doesn't feel that kind of angst anymore and it's enough to relax me, for now.

Dalia steps to the wall of the fenced-in sparring ring for a closer inspection of us and she is openly unimpressed. "Aww, yuh mus be joking... 'dis canno be 'dem!"

Dalia is mid-twenties, lean and thuggish femin-ator with jade-green eyes and a bad attitude. Friend? Enemy? There's no way to be sure. But one thing is obvious—she is the unquestioned leader of this group. Dalia exits the ring and circles us like a wolf squaring off in front of Candace, who instinctively hides behind me for protection. She approaches me and plants her face right in front of mine. I know she expects me to waiver but I refuse to give her the satisfaction.

Jazmine is amused by this game of eye-chicken. "Girl, this one here is tough. You better not cross her," she laughs.

Dalia pulls out a curved blade and stares at it. "Nah, her no craze." She slides the blade across her tongue. "But I iz." Dalia smiles a wicked bloody grin.

I maintain a fixed stare, expecting to hear Candace's body hit the floor at any moment.

"Damn Girl, you've got issues! You're gonna cut that that thing off one of these days." Jazmine decrees.

"Alright, that's enough," Luther declares. "Dalia put the knife away." She reluctantly sheaths the blade. "Well, you've met Dalia," he continues.

"This young lady right here is Ryan, our explosives expert," he presents. The woman Dalia was fighting is Ryan. She's twenty-five and looks like a darker-skinned Jay Lo. She nods her head—"Hey," is all she says.

"That's Jazmine," he advises. "She can drive anything with a motor." Jazzy's a twenty-eight-year-old, athletically built, lady bruiser with a mahogany complexion and shoulder-length hair. She gives him an outrageous mock salute—she's obviously the jokester of the bunch. Even a ninja squad needs one.

Cofaxx then directs our attention to a huge command center, where a petite Caucasian chick pecks away on several keyboards at once. "The bookworm over there is Madison, our resident genius. She has the unique ability to hack into any computer system known to man," Cofaxx tells us.

Madison La Fleur, a.k.a. Skye, is in her early twenties. She's a trendy hipster with glasses and long, flowing brunette hair. She doesn't look up from her command center but she does acknowledge us with an absent wave of her hand.

"Sirens, meet your new teammates," Cofaxx announces. Deseree waves. Candace remains cautious—make that scared shitless. As for me, I keep up my cool defiant 'tude. I don't want these broads' getting any ideas about testing me.

Suddenly, as if shot out of a fairy dart cannon, Madison jumps down from her post to greet us, hugging each of us in a giddy display of pep-squad emotion. "Hi, you guys! It's super nice to meet you. Welcome to the team! If you need anything, just let me know, okay?" she explodes.

"Hey, Snow Flake... chill, Damn!" Jazmine hisses.

"Don't mind them. They're a bunch of kittens, once you get to know 'em," Madison assures.

Cofaxx shows us a man in his late fifties, working on a car in the vehicle bay. He's Charles Scrap—a gentle giant and the Sirens' weapon and mechanic specialist. "Afternoon, ladies," he greets.

Desee studies the group for a moment. "So, you're the genius. You drive, and you blow things up. What do you do?" she interrogates Dalia.

"Me? I jus kill... ery-ting," the bully of a woman answers in her distinct island drawl.

Naturally, I have to wonder where three strippers fit into this misfit group, but I keep my mouth shut.

"Alright, let's get started!" Cofaxx commands.

We are immediately thrust into a world of Mixed Martial Arts, Weapons and Tactics, and Military-style training, the likes of which only a special-forces operative would be privy to. Our days are full of intense conditioning workouts. Cofaxx does crazy shit, like dropping medicine balls on our bare stomachs while we do sit-ups. Shooting high-velocity tennis balls that we're expected to dodge and other demented exercises.

We learn how to escape confinement and leap tall buildings in a single bound. Cofaxx tells us our missions will require every ounce of grit and fight we can muster. He constantly tests the line between control and chaos to find the survivor's instinct buried within each of us.

None of it bothers me. I've been living in fear all of my adult life and I'm just enjoying the idea of how that feeling will soon be history. Cofaxx says we'll train during the day so we can maintain our club jobs at night and avoid suspicion. How or when we'll be able to catch some 'Z's is anyone's guess.

Candace, Deseree, and I quickly learn that the Sirens draw their power from stealth and silence. Cofaxx's ability to inspire and command makes this an easy concept to buy into. The veteran Sirens are also a pretty good advertisement that his methods work.

CHAPTER 11

ALPHA FEMALE

We continue training for weeks. Cofaxx insists that our best offense is the ability to defend ourselves. "Your enemy cannot touch what it cannot see, nor can it catch what isn't there. You are ghosts, ladies," he insists.

Dalia is a beast. I watched her once stand blindfolded beneath a tree with heavy clay vases hanging from its branches. She shattered all of them, using only her feet, without missing a beat. As my rival, she also takes every opportunity she can to challenge me.

So naturally, finally standing there across the Octagon from her, poised in her signature coiled viper stance, I'm clinched tighter than a pretty boy in prison. Dalia grins at me devilishly and I know she's been waiting for this moment since she first set eyes on me.

"Ready? Fight!" shouts Cofaxx. Dalia shuffles around the ring, taunting me. I center myself—waiting. The cheers from the Sirens sound hollow next to the sound of her feet tapping the canvas.

Dalia dives at me in a blur, delivering a flurry of punches, most of which connect. She choke-slams me to the floor; before I figure out what's happening. I would have been content to lay there but as I'm snatched off the ground and tossed into the gate, I realize this nightmare has only just begun.

Dalia flies at me with a knee that I narrowly dodge staggering back to the center of the ring. The bitter taste of blood fills my mouth and I have yet to land a solid punch. Wearily, I chant inside my brain: "Damn it Jeadda, fight!" trying to will myself into attack mode. Alas, I 'm motivated in spirit but not in deed.

I swing wildly but nothing will touch. Before I can recover, she pummels my ribs. For a moment, I can see each punch as it drops and I become aware that she isn't just trying to beat me—she intends to break me!

A blast of adrenaline surges through me and purely by instinct I head butt Dalia in the face, stunning her and causing blood to stream from her nose. The look of utter shock on her face is priceless and for a second, I allow myself to hope for some inconceivable victory scenario.

Those dreams are quickly dashed as Dalia retaliates, striking me several times. She then locks me in a Python chokehold cutting off my air supply. "Jeadda, tap out!" Cofaxx yells, but I refuse. I feel her grip around my throat tighten and then... nothing but darkness.

I awake to the harsh sting of smelling salts in my nostrils. Cofaxx's deep voice sounds miles away. "Jeadda, are you okay?" I sit up and see Dalia talking to Jazmine through the fence—no doubt gloating. She aims that snooty grin of hers at me and suddenly I want to go a few more rounds—well at least in my mind, I do.

"Do you know why you were beaten?" Cofaxx asks me.

"She's a better fighter than me," I grouse.

Cofaxx stares at me like he doesn't believe me. Then he gives me a Yoda look. Uh oh. He's getting ready to deliver some sage bull crap...

"Better, No. Stronger, yes—Faster, perhaps," he says. "But none of that explains why you lost. You feed off of your emotions, Jeadda. They are your gift and your curse. You must learn to control them or they will control you."

What the fuck is all that supposed to mean? I hate when he talks like Mr. Miyagi. Just say 'DUCK!' or 'MOVE YOUR ASS OUT OF THE WAY!!!'

One takeaway from that expert ass-beating is, the determination never to let myself be embarrassed like that again. I make it my business to absorb every bit of teaching I can drag out of our training sessions from then on.

As a newbie, I never question Cofaxx's plan. It's not until Deseree insists, "Enough with this defense stuff. When do we learn how to attack," that I even consider there may be an alternative.

Seeing as how the original Sirens had been kicking our collective asses around the room for weeks, we all should have been naturally inclined to go on the offensive. Are we truly **_that_** used to being victims—like those battered chicks you hear about all the time, defending the dudes that brutalize them?

Instead of being angry, Cofaxx beams at Deseree. "I was beginning to think you'd never ask," he says. I just gasp, wondering how long he would have let us endure this madness if no one had spoken up.

Cofaxx switches our training regimen to a format that promotes offensive combat. Striking, kicking, submission holds—oh my! I **do** declare, it's raining whoop-ass! We even learn something called Pressure-Point-Consideration which graduates us from Prey to Predator status.

Soon, each of us is revealing our own uniquely brutal gifts—something Cofaxx promised would happen as we found ourselves. We also start, despite our individual talents, to function more effectively as a team. Now the Sirens are blessed with Candace, codename Candy, who excels in close-quarters combat. And don't get me started on her knife-throwing skills! Bitch could hit a fly between the 'shit sniffers' at 30 paces. Her speed and ridiculous body control make her both, graceful and deadly.

Deseree, on the other hand, proves to be a natural at long-distance combat—sharpshooting, to be exact. That's her to a T—firing off phallic symbols quicker than a teenage boy can shoot his load—but with elite sniper accuracy.

As for me, training brings out a competitive nature in me I never knew existed. I develop a deep attraction to the Samurai Code of swordsmanship as I slice n' dice my way into Katana warrior rank. I love this style of fighting for its discipline, its deep and ancient tradition, and its soul. However, I'd be lying if I said I'm not also partial to the twin black 9mm Berettas Cofaxx gave me for tight situations. It's hard not to get hooked by both, their sleek beauty and the easy death count they bring!

So, there you have it. JADE. JAZZY. SKYE. RAYNE. CANDY. CHEROKEE. And me—STARR. Now we're ready to begin the task of righting the wrongs within our city. We will extinguish the fears that have run rampant throughout crime-ravaged communities. We will act as Judge, Jury, and Executioner. We are Vengeance personified. WE ARE THE SIRENS!

I soon understand how quickly things happen when you're a ninja-chick. Not even a week later, we are at the Hub finalizing plans for our first official hit. Tomorrow will be the telltale mission that either justifies or delegitimizes all we've been through these past few months. Ever the perfectionist, Cofaxx fine-tunes his checklist for what will be the extermination of a major drug distributor, Ricardo Basil.

This dude is a flashy club owner and playboy type with Mafia aspirations and a dust habit that makes him unpredictable. Rumor has it, that he's ordered his bodyguards to raid several low-rent drug houses for money and of course Blow. At one such crack house, his goons killed several women and children simply because they were, in Ricardo's own words, 'in the way.' What a way to solidify a tough guy Rep.

I notice Scrap and Cofaxx speaking in serious tones, and try my best to listen in. "So, tomorrow's the big day. What do you think?" he asks Cofaxx, in his Dr. Phil way.

"They are ready," Cofaxx assures, even though that isn't really the question Scrap is asking.

"So, killing these men, do you think it's going to make your pain go away?" Scrap probes further. Cofaxx stares into an abyss. "You know, Luther, you could kill every living thing on this planet and it still wouldn't be enough to fill the void of missing her. I loved my niece like she was my very own child... but Lauren is gone, and she isn't coming back. You need to make peace with that, son. Stop chasing the dead or you'll end up right there in the grave with them."

But Cofaxx will not be swayed by any last-minute arguments. His silence is enough of an answer for now.

Scrap sighs in concession. "Well... good talk then."

That night, we all sleep at the Hub—at least, some of us sleep. I study Dalia, peacefully snoozing like she's already won the battle. I close my eyes and try to envision every possible situation and outcome. It seems like only moments have passed until the blaring alarms we've go off around our bunks.

The morning consists of bacon, eggs, and several tactical dry runs in which we try to compensate for Murphy's Law.

By the time night falls again, we know the mission inside and out. There's only one problem, some of us have never actually killed a living, breathing human being before. There's no way to simulate that, I conclude, other than through trial by fire. Suddenly, I get why Cofaxx's defense philosophy is so important to believe in. We're vigilantes; not killer psychos, after all.

Midnight. A colossal silver base-ball of a moon creates shades and shadows. The perfect time for hunting.

The entrance to Ricardo Basil's tacky 'Club Ice' hums with activity. A long line of patrons wraps around the corner. Inside, the club is crammed. This is the kind of place where all the winners of radio contests end up for their reward of cheap booze. Everyone there is trying way too hard—as if to say: Look at me! I'm having sooooo much fun!

Harsh lights flicker and Salsa music blasts relentlessly through massive speakers with feedback pops. A luxury SUV pulls up to the rear entrance, where several other expensive vehicles are parked. Several armed guards stand watch. Gangster types exit their cars and grab duffle bags from the trunks.

Finally, LF12 leader, Cisco emerges and they head for the back door. He is greeted there by a beefy young man named Raymond Costa, who is Ricardo's sidekick. "Cisco, it's good to see you again. The boss, he is expecting you," he says. The men shake hands and Raymond leads the group through the kitchen. Some of the LF12 Gang members wait near the cars.

Generous moments pass and while making small talk with each other about widescreen TVs and badly trained dogs, one gangster notices a tiny red dot positioned on his comrade's chest like a glowing, nocturnal bee.

"What the fuck is that?" he asks. This is the last thing he ever gets to say out loud before his head explodes like a melon. SHOOOP! Deseree, perched on a rooftop, resets her aim and lifts the other man off his feet with a silenced gunshot blasts to his chest. Jazmine adds her firepower to the fray and, between the two of them, the remaining guards are wasted by a series of silenced precision kill shots.

One of the drivers grabs his phone but he's stopped mid-dial when a curvy, shadowed figure steps up to his window and dispatches a single bullet straight through his head.

We regroup on the roof of the club—all except for Deseree, who remains on her perch, and Dalia. "Wait, where's Dalia?" Candace asks as we stare down through the skylight at a room full of totally unsuspecting club-goers.

"Who cares?" I blurt. The ladies reward my comment with withering looks. "Kidding," I relent.

Candace radios Dalia, who is crouched near the back door of the club—peeking through a window. A waitress walks into the office near the door just as Dalia receives Candace's call. "Jade, come in. I repeat—Jade, where are you?"

Dalia answers, reluctantly: "Plan's changed." That's all she says—no explanation, no nothing.

The look on Ryan's face indicates that this is nothing new. "Here we go again," she sighs, checking her clip.

"Can she do that?" Candace helplessly questions.

"She just did... Let's go!" Jazzy instructs.

Cisco and his Guards have reached Ricardo's office.

"Cisco, mi amigo... como estas?" Ricardo greets. He's dressed like Don Johnson from those Miami Vice reruns.

"I am well, my friend. How is business?" Cisco responds.

Ricardo points to a two-way mirror that overlooks his crowded club. "Business, she is fantastic, thanks to you. I've increased my clientele three times over in the past month alone" Ricardo gushes. "Come, I just got a case of Balvene Portwood Scotch in. I'll have my server bring it to us." He pauses, remembering Cisco's legendary OCD. "You do like Scotch, don't you? What am I saying, of course you do!" Poor Ricardo; he just can't tell from Cisco's Prison molded expressions.

By this time, Dalia has entered the back door and made her way inside the small office space. She sets the now unconscious waitress down on the floor. She peeks out of the window to choose who she'll take down next. Suddenly Dalia hears Ricardo's voice on the office intercom: "Send a bottle of the new Scotch to my suite, immediately," he demands. She examines the uniformed waitress and grins deviously.

Upstairs, one of the gangsters unzips a duffle bag and pulls out a brick-shaped package that he hands to Ricardo. The known addict slits open the package with a butterfly blade and scoops out powder which he inhales—rubbing the residue on his gums. "Oh, shit, yeah! That's the magic!" he declares.

There is a knock at the door and a guard opens it. Who should enter but Dalia, disguised in the waitress' uniform? She breezes into the suite and presents drinks to the men. Cisco glances at her suspiciously while Ricardo raises his glass to toast. "To continued success... and excess," he crows.

"Salude," Cisco agrees. The men drain their glasses.

"So, let's talk money," Ricardo begins, but his attention is grabbed by Dalia, still standing there. "What are you waiting for, a tip?"

Dalia grins at him. "No, I just like to watch," she replies.

"Watch what?" Ricardo laughs.

Dalia's grin widens. Without warning, a bullet bursts through Ricardo's head cherry-bomb style spraying brain fragments over Dalia's suit—she isn't fazed one bit. Dalia spins and hurls a knife into a guard's skull. Cisco goes for his weapon but Dalia swiftly kicks the gun out of his hand.

Two more guards are quickly dispatched with silenced rounds and even though they are in close quarters, the remaining protectors begin to shoot wildly. They shatter the window and glass spills into the panicked crowd.

The ladies watch the carnage through modified goggles from their sniper positions. The wall to Ricardo's office crumbles in the hail of gunfire we administer.

POOF POOF POOF! Dalia shoots another guard in his kneecaps, flooring him before slamming her boot heel through his face.

From behind the slightly opened door across the hall, I watch as another guard lumbers up the stairs. He pauses outside the door, hoping to get the drop on whoever is inside. BOOM! He flies into the room full of the buck-shots I've just injected into his chest.

Dalia takes advantage of my surprise entrance by stabbing Cisco in the chest. Without even bothering to pull the knife out, the crazed man lunges at her. "You Bitch!" he bellows.

Dalia peppers the man with jabs that sound like percussion drubs, then in one fluid motion, she snatches the blade from his chest, and slits his throat. If that weren't kick-ass enough, Dalia spin-kicks his drug-pedaling ass through the window. He plummets into the trash behind the bar. It's kind of ironic to think about it, Cisco's last moments dying in a pile of dirty bar rags.

CHAPTER 12

AFTERMATH

We arrive back at the Hub earlier than expected. Madison is at her command center worried sick. Scrap is in the vehicle bay working on one of the cars, while Cofaxx tries in vain to meditate near the ring. He opens his eyes as our SUV screeches into the garage.

Deseree and Candice are somber. Meanwhile, Dalia, Ryan, and Jazmine, undaunted by the craziness of tonight, laugh and joke as if we're returning from a girl's night out. They congratulate Desee on her clutch shooting, and all I can wonder is, are we becoming as dangerous as those we're meant to protect people from? I know they're thinking it. Personally, I have already decided not to care, but it's going to take my soft-hearted friend some time to reconcile things.

"So, things went according to plan, then?" Cofaxx debriefs.

"Whose plan?" I grouse. Dalia shoots me a dirty look, but I don't care—that Lone Ranger shit she pulled put everyone in jeopardy.

"Yah, maan... no worries. We run and gun dem. Deh dinno see nuting," Dalia reports. I'm sure to her, things went just as expected but somehow my preparations never factored in a rogue teammate.

Cofaxx approaches me and puts his hand on my shoulder. "Are you alright?"

"When do we get Dunlock?" I demand.

Cofaxx recoils back to his stoicism. "We will meet T.R.A.P. soon enough. Trust me, we will both have our revenge," he assures me.

Moments later, I find myself in one of the HUB's restrooms; splashing cold water over my face—it shocks my senses but provides no answers to the questions pin-balling inside my brain. When I raise my head again; whose reflection is standing behind me? Dalia is gazing balefully into the glass.

"I donno wha deh el yuh tink dis iz, Barbie, but dis shit inno for play play! Us kill or us dead, dats ih! Don't eva question meh decision again—or I done yuh meh-self," she threatens.

She's gone before I can respond—admittedly, it could have been much worse. Especially with all the metal objects in the room.

The next day, back at the 34th Precinct building, our brave yet clueless Detectives are summoned into the Captain's office to discuss our little party-crasher and understandably it's not a cordial meeting. He holds up a folder full of papers and waves it around.

"Do you know what this is?" he quizzes, slamming the folder down on his desk.

"New sexual harassment policy?" Sonny quips, trying to lighten the mood, but the Captain isn't amused.

"No, Smart Ass, these are forty-seven emails I've received in just this past hour—from the Commissioner to the Mayor biting my damned head off about this crime spike…"

"Captain, we're making progress but these things take time," Arturo clarifies.

"Time? I just got a call from the Governor in Washington DC telling me that, if I don't fix this shit soon, I'm going to be looking for work at the supermarket! So, hear this, you have seventy-two hours to get me some damned results or... or else!"

Under the gun, Arturo decides to move up his scheduled raids on LF12 sites. Team Scorpion converges on an extremely important location that very night—the late Cisco's stash-house. Officers smash through doors, yelling and arresting everyone inside. Soon they have a long line of cuffed gangsters kneeling on the lawn.

"Alright, so who's it gonna be, huh? Who wants to go to jail and who wants to go home?" Arturo asks. "What about you, Esse... you ready to roll homes?"

The gangsters remain silent.

"Oh, come on now; don't everybody speak at once." Arturo approaches grim-faced, bald Latino, Beto Hernandez. "You... what's your name, Vato?" he asks.

"Smokey, Homes," the man answers.

"What do ya say, Smokey... want to save yourself some cell time?"

"Aye yo, fuck you, puto... LF, don't snitch!"

"Come on guys, you think I don't know how this works? Somebody's going to talk, they always do. None of you wants Fed time, right?" Arturo circles the men. "You want to get ass raped? Eat slop and spend twenty-three hours a day in a box? Or do you want to go home? The choice is yours, but the train's pulling outta the station."

Officer Betty Stone, poised line woman looks, catches the Detectives' attention from her position by the front door. "Sirs, I think you're gonna want to see this," she suggests. Arturo and Sonny follow her into the house. They are led to the basement where Mao Lei is being tended to by paramedics.

"Dinh's daughter?" Arturo looks puzzled.

"What's she doing here? I thought the homies were staying out of this feud," Sonny verbalizes his partner's query.

"Looks like they might be the cause of it," Arturo replies.

That bust must've given those cops a much-needed boost of confidence, because the next night they pop up at Club Eye Candy, snooping around like they're regulars or something. Candace is on the main stage, performing when the Detectives enter the club and begin to flash their badges all CSI style. The patrons groan and many of them scoot for the exit.

Sir Monte' watches his cash cows stampede out the door, in dismay. He darts over to his intercom to warn us: "Attention, ladies... we have a Code Blue. I repeat Code Blue... the Bacon is in the pan. Abort all VIP activities immediately."

Sir rushes over to stall the Detectives. "Well, good evening, officers. What brings you by my respectable law-abiding, establishment this evening?"

Sonny guffaws. "Respectable? Man, stop it!"

Sir must stop and breathe through his anger at being ridiculed.

"Sir, we'd like to have a word with an employee of yours, Jeadda Tibbadaux," Arturo explains.

Sir frowns as he searches his mental Rolodex for my government name. I can imagine the 'NO RESULTS FOUND' signal in his brain. It's my fault really—in my attempts to maintain certain boundaries between my two worlds; I had avoided giving him my birth name. I mean, it wasn't like I received a printed paycheck or a 401k Pole Dancer package.

"Jeadda who?" Sir asks. Sonny presents him with my file. "Oh, you mean Starr? Yeah, she's set to go on next. What'd she do?"

"We just need to ask her some questions about the disappearance of Monica Warren," Arturo informs my increasingly uneasy Boss.

"Who? Speak English, Man... I don't know what you're talking about."

Sonny's impatience is now evident. "Damn man, Monica Warren? Hispanic female... twenty-one-year-old, mother of one?" he reminds a blank-faced Sir. "Recently found beaten to death?"

Sir becomes visibly anxious. "Whoa shit, well you know, I don't condone senseless acts of violence in my club. This is a wholesome and God-fearing titty bar... like the ones in Bethlehem," Sir blathers, adding for good measure: "Just so you know, Starr's ass is only part-time here, anyway."

"Easy man, she's not in any trouble," Arturo assures him. "This is just part of our investigation. We're interviewing everyone close to the victim... that's all."

"Yeah, well that's fine. You gentlemen have a seat. I'll have someone bring you a couple of drinks." Sir aims the Detectives in the direction of the bar.

"No thanks, we're on duty. I'll take a Coke though."

Candace, having seen all this, wraps up her routine and heads for the locker room. Bates can't help ogling at her as she scurries passed him. Arturo notices his partner's distraction. "Detective?" he nudges Sonny. "Do you want a soda?"

Sonny declines.

I'm about to go upstairs when Candace skids into the dressing room, spouting off about the arrival of the officers. I have to calm her down, so I can get a coherent report on our upstairs visitors. Although she didn't exactly hear the conversation, Candace is convinced they are here to arrest us.

I instruct my jitter-bug of a friend to stay calm until we know for sure and remind her that, according to Cofaxx, we're contracted by a government agency. I doubt he would let them put us in jail.

Once upstairs, I approach the detectives to see what they know and test my resolve under pressure. Just as I thought, Detective Carone and Bates couldn't be more off-target. They ask me questions about my friendship with Monica and I find out they got my contact info from the papers I had to sign when I identified Monica's body—something told me not to do that shit.

They try to convince me that Monica may have fallen back into using and they grill me about whether or not I knew it. I make sure to let them know in no uncertain terms, that Monica had been through a lot of things in her past but she would never have gone back to that life—she didn't want that.

Candace watches me from a safe distance while giving a half-hearted lap-dance to some severely chubby John with man-boobs—you know the kind that rides around on scooters in Walmart.

After wasting my time, the veteran Detective slides his card my way. "Give us a call if you think of anything that might assist us in this investigation." line.

Candace is still entertaining Bob's-Big-Boy who by this time is sniffing her hair proclaiming, "Mmmm, girl you so soft... and you smell like strawberries and plums and grapes. I could just bite you." Who was this guy fooling?

Once the Detectives depart, Candace rushes over to me sliding to a halt near the bar. She starts carpet-bombing me with WHO, WHERE, WHEN, and WHAT, questions. "So... what did they say? Are we in trouble?"

"Girl, do you see me getting dragged out of here in handcuffs? They just wanted to know about Monica," I assure her. "They call themselves wanting to help."

"It's a little late for all that now," Candace reminds me. She couldn't be more right. We have crossed the point of no return.

CHAPTER 13

DIRECT HIT

The next step of Cofaxx's plan involves gaining Intel from a high-ranking member of The Family—preferably someone not so high up the chain of command that they will arouse suspicion. Enter, Victor Poullo, the Don's Nephew by marriage and a total screw-up by nature. His big mouth and flashy antics have embarrassed the Don on more than one occasion, but lately, he's been off the grid—mostly held up in a suite at The Four Seasons. The idea is to catch him and 'convince' him to roll on his Uncle.

Maxine Carver, a highly paid, bouncy red-headed escort, has been seen 'cumming' and going from his room on a fairly regular basis. One morning as she finishes up her session with Victor and accepts his generous 'gift' we set out to infiltrate. She exits the suite, then turns back and kisses Victor. "Mmm, I had a real good time, Baby."

"Yeah, then this should be free, right?" Victor may be wealthy but he's also a notorious cheapskate.

"Aww, baby, a girl's got to pay the rent, doesn't she?" Maxine prods him. "But call me soon and we'll hang out again, okay?" She snatches the wad of cash from his hand, then turns and walks towards the elevators, passing some guards he has stationed in the hall.

Maxine steps into the elevator; and is startled by the unexpected presence of Dalia, dressed in what I can only describe as 'tough chick trendy' attire—camouflage pants, a wife-beater T-shirt, that accentuates her impressive rack.

Dark shades cover her eyes allowing her to scope out the guards without detection. Maxine fixes her hair in the poor reflection of the metal walls. "Can you believe how cheap the guys in this city are?" she asks Dalia.

"Yah-mon."

After sizing up Maxine, Dalia decides once again to deviate from the original plan and make things more interesting for herself.

One awkward ride later, the elevator reaches the ground floor. "Take it easy out there, Honey," Maxine suggests quickly exiting the elevator—after a moment, Dalia follows.

Maxine lights a cigarette as she walks, completely unaware she is being stalked. Just as the call-girl reaches her car, parked underneath the hotel, Dalia grabs her and sticks the curved knife to her throat.

"Yuh scream, mi a slit yuh troat… unnastan?"

Maxine whimpers and nods in agreement. "Good Gyal, now me gon ask yuh dis wan time, an' yuh betta give it tuh meh straight. Who ya workin' fir?"

"M-M-Madam LeDea. Elite Escorts. Please don't kill me… I've got a kid."

Dalia's lip sneers. "Yuh wirk feh mi now, yuh hir?"

Maxine nods.

While Dalia continues to have her fun spooking the escort, the rest of us are busy at the Hub—worrying our weaves lose. Of course, we're still unaware that she's ignoring our best-laid plans—**_again!_**

Scrap invites me to take a sneak peek at a swivel holster modification thingy he's been working on—patent pending. He clips the attachment to his belt and holsters a pistol in it. The mechanism allows him to literally shoot from the hip, without even drawing the weapon. 'Wow! I'm glad he's on our side,' is my only thought.

Candace is in the Octagon, swinging and kicking at a pad Cofaxx holds. He shouts, "Faster... Harder... Faster, Candace... Harder! Don't quit... Don't give up!"

I return my attention to Scrap—well sort of. "Hey, let me ask you something. You've known Cofaxx for a long time, right? What's his story?" I ask, figuring if anyone would know, it would have to be a relative.

"His... is a sad story," Scrap sighs. "But it's not my place to tell."

I accept his code of silence begrudgingly and stop prying.

OM to the G, has it seriously been a week since our first raid? I find myself craving a quick fix of danger like an adrenaline-tweaker. As Arturo suspected, several of the gangsters were ultimately willing to cooperate with the police investigation in exchange for leniency.

The Scorpion Task Force has also been busy, busting up small drug spots around the city. On one otherwise still night however, they separate into strike teams to go for a big bust, at an LF12 Heroin manufacturing plant, disguised as an auto restoration business at the edge of the Castro clicks territory.

Arturo leads the group; positioning his Alpha Team a block away from the entrance. Bravo Team is closer and assigned to breach detail. The Scorpions maintain constant radio contact and although night has just fallen and the area is cleared of civilians, no one expects an easy go of things.

Arturo verifies positions and prepares to strike but just before he can give the go-ahead, the cars parked around the facility begin to explode! Gunfire erupts inside the warehouse, followed by the ear-splitting pop of grenades. It sounds like the War on Terror has been unleashed state-side.

See, little do the Scorpion members know, a certain ragtag group of female assassins has also been planning a raid on that same warehouse. If the cops hadn't been pushed to speed up their operation; this place would have been a smoking crater by the time they touched down. As it stands, we've already breached the building and are laying waste to the entire Horse farm. Gangsters and manufacturers scatter from the building, some on fire even, adding to the chaos.

Arturo has no choice but to call for an emergency breach of the building. One of the armored Scorpion vans smashes through the entrance gate, followed by the Bravo Team. The sniper team unleashes a hail of bullets at the baddies from key positions. Alpha Team moves in with military precision. Moments later, the sound of internal gunfire suddenly ceases, leaving a jarring silence. Arturo flashes hand signals and the team bursts into the facility.

The two teams carefully secure the warehouse—not that there's much of anyone left to resist. These brash enforcers seem mystified to find a decimated chemical lab filled with pre-packaged narcotics, smashed drug equipment, thousands of shell casings, and enough bodies to choke a crematorium. All in less than 3 minutes.

Suddenly, Joker emerges from an office, bleeding profusely and aiming a pistol in the air. His shifty eyes gaze at the dark corners unconcerned with the officers—there's something even scarier than 'the fuzz' lurking in the shadows. "Where the fuck, are you, mother fucker!" he yells.

Arturo aims his gun at Joker's head. "Drop your weapon or I'll end you! Hey... look at me!" Joker's eyes glance reluctantly. "Drop it, now," the Detective demands.

Joker finally notices the officers surrounding him and he drops his weapon. "Help me, man... you gotta help," he pleads, but before he can finish his thought a bullet cuts straight through his throat silencing the man for good—a snitches reward. The officers are sprayed with neck juice and Joker is a memory before he hits the ground.

Arturo and his team take cover but whoever just dropped Joker has no interest in killing cops. He observes a pair of legs disappearing through an open panel in the roof.

Suddenly, a frantic call blares through the radio. Sargent Mannie Stuart, one of the Delta Team Snipers barks in panic: "I've got multiple hostiles!" He is cut off by a kick to the face from one of the assailants, and Arturo dispatches men to the rescue.

"Alpha team, I want you to set up a perimeter. No one gets in or out," Carone orders. "Bravo team, find Sgt. Stuart!" They charge off. "Bates, you're with me... hope you like climbing, partner."

Sonny is once again forced to combat his fear of heights as they scale a ladder toward the roof.

The two detectives emerge onto the roof into the bracing night air. Reluctantly splitting up, to cover more ground, they search for their mysterious assassin. Sonny eases around a corner and is attacked by a masked figure dressed in black combat gear. The assailant slams him onto the roof siding with a surplus of stealth and skill. The tiny villain pulls out an equally small sword and places it at the cop's corroded artery.

Sonny doesn't flinch. "GO AHEAD. WHAT ARE YOU WAITING FOR... DO IT!!! The ninja stares at him curiously. He pulls back his sword and darts towards the edge of the roof.

From his position, Arturo spots the ninja and gives chase. "Freeze... don't make me shoot you!" he shouts and is relieved when the killer stops just short of the ledge. The ninja turns to face him. Even as a grizzled vet, Arturo has never experienced anything quite like this. 'This guy's got major Huevos rancheros.'

"Stop... you just stop! It's over alright... there's nowhere left to run," Arturo advises, slowly inching his way closer to the dark figure. "Lie face down on the ground, and spread your arms out to the side." Just then, the chatter begins to bleed into his headset—one of the snipers,

Patrick Smart, positioned on a rooftop across the way, has the Ninja in his sights.

Without warning the ninja hurls the sword at the Detective, then dives off of the building—gracefully falling backward just as--

BOOM!

The Scorpion sniper fires. "Direct hit... I got him!" Arturo hears officer Smart, crow into the com.

Sonny joins Arturo, and the two Detectives rush downstairs expecting to find a dead or at least badly wounded ninja. Once at the ground level they discover that the assailant has vanished and there is nothing—not even a drop of blood to verify he was even there. "Negative... that's a negative on the target. We got nothing," reports the bewildered Lead Detective on his radio.

An officer, hands Arturo the sword from the wall it was buried in, and he is prompted to assume the seemingly obvious. "A damned short-sword! It's gotta be the Yukoshi right?" Sonny lobbies. But something doesn't feel right.

"I'm not so sure anymore... there's something about this... something familiar," Arturo insists, to no one in particular. He's never liked riddles, and he's just been handed a hell of a big one.

Come to think of it... why did the assassin deliberately miss him with the blade? And why did all of his mysterious cohorts spare the Scorpions? They only seemed interested in the gang bangers.

Sure, Arturo is asking the right questions. Too bad he and his hoity-toity special task force are so far from the answers. Yup! Too bad... ***for them!***

The police know that there's a war being waged in the streets and they may even know the major players involved but they never accounted for the possible presence of another team of heroes, they never expected—The Sirens.

CHAPTER 14

CROSSING THE LINE

How, you must be wondering, did the ninja survive the fall and escape undetected?

All is answered when a, very familiar, SUV pulls to a stop near an alley a mile away from the raid site. The aforementioned ninja hobbles out from the shadow of the buildings toward it. Can you believe it, the assassins who were handing out fresh ass-kickings moments earlier; were a bunch of chicks! We emerge from the vehicle and collect our teammate.

Removing the mask reveals Ryan, and she's been shot in the back by some prick Cop! She cries out in excruciating pain.

"Drive!" I yell and Jazmine speeds off.

"That asshole shot me! I can't believe he shot me!" Ryan whimpers in disbelief.

I don't blame her for being surprised. Anonymity has its issues the most crucial of course being, the distinct possibility of getting shot. It's a valuable lesson and reminds us that we are still mere mortals. I just didn't want Ryan to pay the price for it.

Deseree screams for Ryan to breathe. Candace screams that we should get her to a hospital and I'm not exactly sure what to scream.

Jazmine nixes that whole hospital idea immediately asserting, "A hospital... and tell them what? Our assassin friend was injured in a raid we just pulled?"

Deseree tries to calm Ryan by stroking her hair, while Jazmine weaves through traffic hoping not to draw attention. In all the chaos, I happen to glance at Dalia, who fiddles with her weapon, completely unbothered by the gravity of the situation. For a moment, I'm entranced watching her aggressively ignore our injured comrade, coldly demanding that: "Sum'ady shut har up!"

It's baffling to me—but thinking back, I'm not sure why. My furious glare in her direction would have melted the face off an actual human being, but Dalia simply puts on her earphones, leans back, and closes her eyes. Murder makes her a tad weary, I guess.

Finally, we pull into the HUB's vehicle bay. Deseree, Candace and Jazmine scream for help and Scrap soon appears. I impulsively look for Cofaxx, like seeing him will fix things. Even in my distracted state, I still hear Scraps roaring in the distance. "Ryan! Ryan! Hold on, baby girl!"

Madison emerges from the sleeping quarters and meets us in the infirmary. "Put her on the table, hurry!" she instructs and Scrap obediently lays Ryan on a metal gurney.

Cofaxx surfaces from his office. "What's wrong... Jazmine, what happened?" he croaks, in a deeply pained voice.

Dalia stands near the vending machine, munching on the candy bar she just swiped. "Me tink har forgot tuh duck," she tells Cofaxx, who doesn't appreciate her sense of humor.

Ryan cries out again while Madison gingerly probes her back for the bullet. "It's too deep... I can't get to it. I'm going to have to use the tongs," she announces.

"Can't you give her something for the pain?" Deseree begs.

"She's lost too much blood. I can't risk it."

She lays her hand on Ryan's head. "Ryan, Sweetie, I'm going to have to pull out the bullet, so I need you to be very still for me, okay? This is going to hurt."

Ryan snivels and nods bravely. Deseree grabs Ryan's hand and gives her a bandana to bite down on. Cofaxx and Scrap hold the sweat-drenched woman down and I grab her feet.

Madison picks a long pair of forceps. "Okay, here we go."

She digs the metal tool into Ryan's back and her muffled screams echo throughout the HUB. Jazmine looks away. Deseree continues to stroke Ryan's hair.

"Almost got it... just a little more..."

By this time, Ryan is so exhausted, she can no longer scream. She loses consciousness, and... "Got it!" Madison reports pulling the metal piece from Ryan's back and dropping it into a tray with an unnerving 'clank!'

Later that night, after Ryan's been stabilized, I notice Deseree watching her sleep—that's it, just watching her. I don't know what to make of it at first, but the more I think about it, I realize that I too am starting to feel differently about this whole Sirens group.

I suppose it's the reason for my strange attachment to Cofaxx—the Sirens have provided me—all of us, with something we've been searching for. These girls aren't just my Teammates, they're my Sisters, my Family. I have grown to care for them, cheer for them, and fear for them—even Dalia. The revelation makes my heart skip a beat. Suddenly, I have a lot more to live for—and a lot more to lose.

Days later, Maxine, calls Candace's cell phone looking for 'Jade'. The devious grin plastered across Dalia's face speaks volumes—as the call girl announces an upcoming date with Victor. The rest of us assume it's her way of getting the Intel we need from him. None of us has a clue that this crazy little trickster plans something more.

That same night, after the ladies have gone to sleep, I'm awakened by an odd, pounding sound. I trail the noise down the hall to the gym and happen upon Cofaxx, wailing away on the heavy bag. I watch for a while as he lands brutal blows.

With each strike, I hear low, stifled groans, and drawing closer, I detect tears streaming from his eyes. He drops to his knees drained by utter despair. Every part of my soul aches at the sight of his grief and I find myself yearning to go to him—comfort him—to touch him.

Before I can check myself for loose screws, I drift over, unnoticed. As I stand behind him, I can feel my instincts taking over—just like on stage. I reach out to him helplessly, trying to figure out what my body will do next. Cofaxx snaps around and grabs my arm—prepared to strike!

When he sees it's me, Cofaxx crumbles at my side wrapping his massive arms around my waist, and buries his face into my thigh. Although every rational part of me tells me I'm about to make a big mistake, I have no control, but to demand: 'Shut the fuck up, brain!' Instead, I listen to my heart. I kiss the tears from his eyes. Apparently, it's been so long since he's felt the tender touch of a woman that the sensation of my lips sends electric charges through him and he seems to savor each one.

I assume that I will be taking the lead and I have absolutely no problem with that, but as I begin my exploration, his giant hands pull me onto the floor. The man savagely rips my shirt apart like it never existed and runs his strong, square hands over me as his eyes bore into mine, revealing years of caged desire. He sucks on my skin and I shake violently consumed by a similarly frantic lust.

Cofaxx inhales and breathes out steamy air that warms my body. My nipples stiffen as he suckles them. If he only knew what that does to me, he might never stop. Cofaxx trails down my stomach with his tongue and yanks my bottoms off in one swift motion—great idea to go bare butt tonight, I commend myself. He pauses in awe at the gushing fountain between my thighs. My pussy lips pulsate and the air becomes thick with our sweet passion.

The man plunges his tongue deep into my reservoir, drinking me. Wave after orgasmic wave crashes onto the shore of his lips. God, I want this so bad it hurts—I need to give him every last drop of me. I struggle to find something to grab on to and I end up biting down on my own arm as I explode, into his mouth. It is all I can do to keep my screams in check and not wake everybody up.

He won't stop tapping my 'open' button with his insanely gifted tongue, until—a gush of warm lust spills out of me. I cover my mouth to suppress yet another monstrous groan as my lady-liquid drains out. By now I am seeing stars and his grip around my thighs tightens. I lie there partly comatose but my toy soldier isn't finished with me just yet.

He rises to his knees and peels the sweaty shirt from his chiseled frame. Then, with his eyes fixed on mine, he unties the drawstring on his pants and unfurls his flag. It is the most magnificent piece of man meat I've ever seen; a torpedo cased in black velvet. He smiles politely, and then climbs on top of me, and gently enters my still pulsing 'cookie.' I gasp, as he pushes inside me, slowly, testing and teasing to see if I can take it all. I am proud to say I do not disappoint.

With every thrust, I feel him igniting fireworks within me as his muscular arms flex like the gears on a giant machine. He flips me over and drives that huge rod once more into my tight hole. I beat my fist against the mat and beg him not to stop as the excruciatingly delicious pain increases.

I fight the urge to tell him I love him. He nuzzles his face in my neck and finally climaxes; loosening his merciless hold on me. I suddenly realize that without question, this has to be the most amazing sexual experience of my young life. Yeah, I tear up a little—don't judge me! This is something I've only heard about from those older, more experienced women, describing their elaborate sexual escapades.

I'm reminded of the words from my favorite erotic writer:

ENCOUNTER

By: DJM

This is between you and me; between the sheets
where passions and pleasures meet
to discuss lengthy hot sessions and shared affections
reflected through reflections of bodies wrecking.
While candle light from candles lit—
dances, enhances, enchanted glances of romantic magic.

Bodies in sync with each other.
Smothered lovers under the covers.
Your tears, my sighs, your moans, and my replies—
And your eyes tell no lies, gazing deeply into mine.

Heavy-breathing, biting like we're teething
proceeding, nails piercing, flesh bleeding.
Needing me, repeatedly repeating my name, again and again,
and I gladly accept the blame of critical acclaim.
Felt your tender pain each time you came
and I felt the same—

As toes curl and eyes clinch;
as mouths part and muscles tense.
Suspended in suspense for each moment after this,
The stars, moons, planets, and constellations
patiently wait in our favor
as each of 69 flavors of sex is sexually savored.

Tastes too tasty to resist revisits visions of bliss,
like at the beginning of this.
The first kiss, the next touch,
that next word meant so much—
told me 'YES', that we could, and we both understood
what that meant.

So, we took the next step,
intimately introducing introductions in depth,
and then conveniently forgetting the rest
as we slept."

We collapse in a haze of fatigue.

No words are spoken—none need to be. Our encounter is perfect just as it is. Neither of us wants to make any assumptions about it, one way or the other.

CHAPTER 15

GIRL FIGHT

So, what I've determined is that Dalia likes to see things unfold up close and personal. I think it reassures her when she can control events and confirm that all of the right people have been punished. That's why she's the one most likely to deliver justice directly to Death's doorstep.

It's not far-fetched at all to imagine her exiting an elevator and strutting her way down a hall at the posh Four-Seasons the next night. I can picture her, in my grey pea-coat and sexy high heeled boots—I mean, let's not get it twisted, she totally has the body to pull that sort of thing off. As the story goes, she is greeted by two of Victor's goons who demand to know who she is.

"Jade... meh wit Elite Escorts," she answers.

"Where's the regular girl?" one of them asks.

"Meh dunno... gyal problems. Yuh gun lemme tru or no?" The men look at one another suspiciously. Dalia's impatience is evident. "No worry, I go? You can splain-a Bictor why." She turns and begins to walk back to the elevator.

"Wait!" one of them calls to her. She grins to herself never having doubted it. Men—they always overlook the little things.

They allow Dalia to pass. She knocks on the door of Victor's suite and then shoots the larger, balder Shrek of a guard, a wink. Victor, wearing a lounge coat, appears from behind the door. He stares blankly at her and then passed her.

"Umm, who are you supposed to be?"

"Jade."

"Okay, Jade... where's Maxine?"

Dalia opens her jacket to show off her sexy physique and lingerie. "Sometin' came up, her canno mek ih. Madam LeDea tawt yuh might like meh insted," Dalia explains.

At the sight of Dalia's flawlessly toned body complete with a full six-pack Ab set, Victor's concern quickly evaporates—and thanks to the 'Blue Bombers' he's been popping like M&Ms another part of him has contracted a sudden spell of rigor mortis. Victor catches Dalia eyeing his side-kick—no sense in letting that go to waste. "Well, you snooze you lose, am I right?" he laughs, stepping aside to usher her in.

That night finds Candace, Deseree, and I back at Eye Candy. I'm preparing for my moment on stage—at the same time feeling rather vexed. There was a point when I could easily have walked away from this entire vendetta madness but now, I'm in waist-deep. I mean, how do I just forget the things I've seen and done? How do I square that without finishing what I started? The thought of it summons migraine symptoms and I breathe deeply hoping to calm myself. What brought this mini anxiety attack on you may ask? I'm staring right at it--

It seems to be gazing right back up at me, daring me to ignore it—an invitation to an upcoming audition for the 'Constance Fairchild Dance Company'. I've been holding on to it for weeks now. To say this opportunity is huge doesn't do it justice. It only happens once a year and the submission process is grueling—and let's just say this is not my first time trying. This could be a game-changer for me—finally a chance to perform with a legit company. It leaves me with a mix of excitement and insecurity.

I'm no dummy; I'm a realist and I know that things have changed. This is no longer an option for me. I swallow the idea hard and fold the letter up hiding it back in my purse just as Candace waltzes into the dressing room. "Dang, these guys sure are grabby, tonight. I have to catch myself so I don't scissor-kick one of these ass-holes," Candace chuckles. "What you doing, Jea?"

"Nothing... just getting ready to go up," I verify, quickly gathering my things before she can get to asking too many questions about how I feel or whatever...

"Well, you watch yourself out there," she warns heading for the showers.

Nope, it's far too late to turn back now—now that I've sacrificed my friends to this grudge, I'm responsible for their safety. They had my back and now I gotta have theirs, even to the death. I march begrudgingly upstairs to thrill my waiting fans—hashtag PISSED!

Cofaxx sits in a limo outside an expensive Hotel somewhere downtown, speaking with our 'financial backer'. The ladies know only that this man is some Government official with major pull.

"I must commend your recent work, Mr. Cofaxx. Your team is most effective," he confesses.

"Yes sir, they are," Cofaxx returns. The man is silent and Cofaxx finds himself waiting for the other shoe to drop.

"Then again, their exploits have generated a great deal of controversy for my department. I don't like having to answer the questions they seem to be triggering," the man continues.

Cofaxx immediately goes on the defensive. "All due respect, Sir... my team is doing the job that no other bureau has been able to do. This war will soon be over and the city will have you to thank for our success."

Cofaxx has little patience for the complaints of those directly benefitting from the services his team provides, without lifting so much as a finger. Then again this is how business is conducted in a Capitalist society—even the business of Justice for Hire...

"Be that as it may, Mr. Cofaxx, the Sirens need to wrap it up. We are growing impatient."

The nerve of this Bozo. I mean the whole reason those Government pen-pushers turned to Cofaxx for help in the first place is that things were getting so bad, they would've had to declare Martial Law. In the land of the free and the home of the brave, that kind of publicity would be detrimental to the city's confidence in the government's ability to protect. It would have been pure chaos and Cofaxx knows it...

"Sir, yes Sir," he grunts as he exits the limo. It's a bitter pill to swallow but nothing worth getting into an argument about.

Days later, Freddy, furtively calls Arturo from a payphone outside of a neighborhood fast-food joint. "San Francisco P.D... Detective Carone speaking," the cop answers.

"Yeah man, it's me, Freddy. I got some information you might be interested in," he says.

"Alright Fred, information like what?"

"Freddy tells the Detective about an interesting conversation he had the previous night. He had been out partying when he was introduced to an African guy. This dude was talking about how his crew is gonna take over the dope game and had shown him a mini-sized menu. It had every kind of drug he had access to, along with their prices. 'I mean, real prices, with... like sales tax and shit.'

Freddy tells Arturo that the man claims to be a part of the T.R.A.P. He brags that he had even gotten the man's bogus business card. The name on the card is Occour Pentae, but Freddy remembers that the man kept calling himself Reese.

By the next morning, the girls and I are growing concerned—we still haven't heard anything from Dalia and are all basically living at the HUB now. Jazmine suggests we call to check on her which of course is tricky because her mission requires her to stay in character.

Ultimately, we decide that Madison has the most inconspicuous voice of all of us, so she should make the call. But what would the ploy be? We threw out everything from Telemarketer to Donation Collector and I think someone even suggests, Grandmother—probably Candace.

Now, what we don't know is that Dalia is relaxing on a couch in Vick's suite, eating an apple and watching cartoons on a large LCD television set. She slices into the apple with her curved blade and laughs at the program. The call finally comes through:

"Who dis?" she answers.

"Umm, Jade... are you okay?" Madison whispers.

Dalia looks at the phone. "White Gyal? Me fine. Wha'ya want?"

"How is your date going?"

"Oh, him dinna wan play nice. So, meh play rough."

Dalia looks across the couch, where Victor is now sitting with his throat slit from ear to ear. His guards also lay dead on the floor, one of them under her feet—a convenient footstool.

Dalia tells us that Victor didn't want to talk so she made sure he'd never speak again. We all assume she didn't give him much of an opportunity.

"Are you still there? Are you coming back soon? Are you going to..." Mildly annoyed, Dalia hangs up before Madison can finish. She offers the corpse a bite of her apple. No response—so she shrugs, continues to eat, and enjoy her program.

When the little old housekeeping spinster arrives at Victor's suite later that day, she is terrified by the sight of Dalia's handiwork. The detectives arrive to investigate and as they stare at Victor's body, Sonny admits that he's getting tired of smelling dead mobster guys.

"It's all part of the chase," Arturo cryptically offers.

"Chase? I only want to chase things I can catch," Sonny replies.

"Guess that rules out women," Arturo quips. A brief moment of lucidity, then it's back to business.

"This doesn't look like any normal hit," he asserts.

Sonny looks around at the candles and rose petals strewn around the room. "Yeah, it looks like Prom Night in here." Both of their faces search aimlessly for a reasonable scenario.

"Alright, I want this place tagged and bagged... there's gotta be some prints. Do we have any witnesses?" Arturo, questions.

"Besides the two guards... Nope. Housekeeper found them this afternoon," Sonny reports.

As the detectives exit the room Arturo notices the security camera and points to it. "What about the security feed?"

"I'm on it," Sonny assures him, making a call to the front desk.

The Detectives view the footage and it does not disappoint, showing Victor receiving regular visits from Maxine with the exception of his final night on earth. It also shows the Guards rushing into his suite at some point—but Dalia is never identified. After Dalia has gone, a bulky man, Giovoni Soro, the Don's man-at-arms, is caught on camera entering the room. Not long after, he leaves in haste.

"Whoa, that's Giovonni," Sonny whistles. "What's he doing there?"

"Looks like, he's igniting a turf war."

"Yeah, but I don't get it. Why knock off your own men?"

To Arturo, Giovanni's motives make perfect sense. Who stands to gain the most if the Don's successors get clipped? And who else can get that close to them? At the end of the day, I guess a cop would know better than anyone else that there really is no honor among thieves.

That morning, Giovonni visits Don Diamante at his Mansion to deliver the news of his nephew's demise, in person. The Don, in the middle of his daily massage, is less than happy to hear the circumstances by which Victor died. It's not that he holds any affection for Victor, but if someone was going to shut that arrogant meatball up, he would have preferred to have given the order himself. Now, there is no telling what this cowardly wretch might have spilled or to whom.

"Son of a bitch! God damn China-men don't learn? Alright then, I'm just gonna have to turn the heat up on those slanty-eyed rice niggers!" he vows.

Giovonni remains unsure that Nu Dinh is the culprit behind this hit. Something about it doesn't seem right.

"Thing is, Boss, I don't think it was the Asians did this. I mean, the room looked like a broad was there—rose petals and candle shit all over the place."

The Don side-eyes his Guard skeptically, and why not? I mean seriously, think of what he was suggesting. "What are you saying to me? You want me to believe some God damn broad did this?" the Don clarifies.

"I'm just saying how it looked, Boss. His neck was cut but, nothing was taken, and I found this." Giovonni hands the Don, Victor's cell phone. "Vick's last call was to his tart, Maxine."

Another long day at the Hub and for the most part I've managed to avoid a physical confrontation with Dalia since she returned from Los

Angeles. Instead, I've focused on becoming faster and stronger, acting and reacting, trusting my instincts... yet still, I can feel her watching me. Next time, I'll be ready for her...

Okay so, I have to admit: 'Next Time' came a little sooner than I expected. We take to the Octagon in an unspoken personal challenge. But now I'm skilled in Kung Fu, Taekwondo, Jujutsu, Judo, Aikido, Muay Thai, and about a dozen other fighting styles. Cofaxx yells: "Fight!" and I attack in a whirlwind of punches and kicks most of which Dalia is able to block or dodge. However, my last kick hits her square in the face.

Dalia retaliates but she cannot connect. I'm too fast for her; too strong. And I've studied her moves too well. We strike at one another in the middle of the ring, but she can no longer penetrate my defenses.

I deliver several staggering hammer blows and am able to pin her against the cage, pummeling her mid-section. I kick and smack her ass all around that ring, but part of me is holding back. In truth, I really don't want to hurt the girl. Just when I think I have her beaten, she twists around and puts me in a headlock. I can't breathe—I can't believe this is happening, again.

At that moment, I remember something Cofaxx said. I must control my emotions or they will control me. I steady my breathing and calm myself, even as Dalia struggles to tighten her grip. I force my fingers under her arm and pull her head into my shoulder to smother her airway. Furious, she lets go with a huff.

I recover with a newfound swag in tow—dancing around the ring, looking for an opening. Dalia retreats into a defensive posture. I watch, amused, while her anger wars with her doubt.

Dalia charges forward and we trade blows, kicks, and backflips. The Sirens cheer us on in this no-holds-barred street brawl. I employ a Kimora Hold on Dalia, ruthlessly tightening my clutch until—I force her to tap out. We stand and bow towards one another and at that moment, Dalia acknowledges my victory with a nod of respect. With that, I take my position as Alpha-female.

I'm not sure exactly what this means as far as our rivalry goes, but I don't care. For me, this is an opportunity to rediscover myself. I am slowly regaining the life that was stolen from me and I'm cherishing every second. Yes, I am finally living up to my true potential.

CHAPTER 16

STUDENT VS. TEACHER

For the time being, the violence plaguing our city has calmed, but we all secretly know we can't afford to relax. The return of Mao Lei was cause for much rejoicing over in the Dinh camp. Nu and his sons resume a host of community projects to mask their criminal doings.

Rumors of a vigilante Death Squad exacting judgment on local criminal organizations have also prompted the Don to adopt a low-key profile. *Hah! 'Vigilante Death Squad.'* That's what the papers calls us. Instead of being appalled, we adopt the handle, along with the subsequent terror from baddies our press must generate. I have to say, things are going well.

So naturally, when the detectives arrive outside of the HUB, late one afternoon, I figure the other shoe has finally dropped and the jig must be up. Madison sees Arturo and Sonny on our security monitors as they pull up and warns Cofaxx. He isn't concerned—as a matter of fact, he appears to be slightly amused. We kick it into high gear, transforming the Hub into a seemingly ordinary MMA gym before letting them in.

Back outside, Arturo presses the intercom call button. "May I help you?" Scrap answers from the command center.

"Detectives Carone and Bates, San Francisco P.D."

"One moment." Moments later, Scrap emerges from the front door of the facility, where the Detectives have been impatiently waiting.

"We're here to speak with Luther Cofaxx," Arturo alerts.

"He's in the middle of a class. Is he expecting you?" Scrap intends to stretch out this greeting as long as he possibly can.

"Does it matter?" Sonny interjects, flashing his badge.

"Guess not. Come on in, Gentlemen." Scrap allows the duo inside and leads them to the gym. Cofaxx is 'conducting' a rudimentary self-defense class and we Sirens are seated on the mat receiving instruction—not to mention, acting our asses off. I get up to assist Cofaxx in the role of his innocent mugging victim. Cofaxx holds me in his Herculean arms and I feel the rhythmic thud of his heart between my shoulder blades. I yearn to be alone with him so I can turn this into a sexy role-play scenario.

The detectives and Scrap enter disturbing his counterfeit lesson. "Cofaxx? You have visitors," Scrap informs.

Arturo steps forward. "Sorry to interrupt, Ladies. My name is Detective Arturo Carone and this is my partner, Detective Sonny Bates." He smiles paternally at us. "I won't take up too much of your time—I just need to have a word with Luther." I pause when I hear him address Cofaxx by his first name. That's a privilege reserved only for the closest of associates.

"Arturo and I were partners on the force, some years back," Cofaxx explains. We look at each other, surprised: Our fearless leader is truly a man of mystery! "I'll be back shortly ladies." Arturo leaves Sonny in the gym and trails Cofaxx into his office.

"How's everyone doing today?" Sonny nervously greets.

No response. 'This boy is in for an awkward time, trying to be coy with the likes of us.' Besides, we're too busy trying to behave like normal chicks, just hanging out with other normal chicks. Under any other circumstances, our situation might be funny.

"Alright, solid," Sonny says accompanied by an awkward 'Black Power' fist gesture.

The way Dalia's eyes dagger at him, tells me it's just a matter of time before she tells the oblivious gum-shoe exactly what we've been doing and dares him to try and stop us.

Meanwhile, I catch Candace making googly eyes at him. And he is quick to flash a killer grin her way, too. "Hey, you look familiar... have we met before?" he asks.

Candace, Olympic Gold-winning tease that she is, shamelessly replies: "No, I doubt it." I silently chuckle.

'Funny how things change when you just add alcohol and stir.'

"Oh, you're probably right. If we had met, I'm sure *you'd* remember it," Sonny asserts. I mean, he actually said that shit, and with a straight face, no less. I'm too through and am just waiting to see Candace shut him down.

Candace, however, starts to giggle helplessly. "Nice save, detective."

"Wait I've got way better stuff than that..." he assures her.

"I bet you do," Candace retorts. By this time, I'm fighting against my gag reflex.

"Seriously though, I was just looking for a way to tell you how beautiful I think you are, without sounding cheesy," he admits with genuine warmth.

'TOO LATE!' I blurt in my head, hoping I can get the words to come out of Candace's mouth, but no such luck.

"You think so, huh?"

"Oh yeah, if it wasn't for that crooked eyebrow, you'd be perfect." Candace, can't help but giggle as she playfully slaps his arm. This time, Sonny looks at her meaningfully and they share a smile.

Meanwhile, inside Cofaxx's office, Arturo tries his best to solicit his former partner's assistance, declaring: "The reason I'm here is because of this drug war—it's brought out some old friends of ours."

Cofaxx leans back in his leather office chair, unimpressed. "So, you want my advice on bringing down Dunlock?

"I mean, you tracked him longer and got closer than anyone's ever been."

"Detective, my search for my brother ended long ago. I have no desire to dredge up old feuds," Cofaxx sighs.

"I understand. It's just that... I know what he took from you..."

"Do you Detective? **_Do you know_** what was taken from me?"

An awkward pause follows. Old partners, yes—and old friends, but certain lines should never be crossed. Arturo realizes his mistake.

"Perhaps I should go... you have my number," he reminds Cofaxx and gets up to leave stopping just short of the door. "Oh, one more thing, there's a rumor going around about a group of vigilante crime fighters... military trained, fast, and deadly. Word is, they belong to Dunlock. What do you make of that?"

"I'm sure I do not know, Detective," Cofaxx offers with studied indifference.

"It's probably nothing. Good seein' you again, Luther."

Back in the gym, Sonny is handing Candace his card. Arturo emerges from the office.

"Bates, let's go!"

"It was nice to meet you, Detective Bates," Candace purrs at Sonny.

"The pleasure was all mine," Sonny confesses. By the look in Candace's eyes, I can tell the Detective has made an impression. It's too bad he's a damn Cop.

I realize that Candace may have inadvertently given us a buffer. There's no way a Detective would knowingly try to date a suspect. I watch her pocket his card. "So, what are you going to do with that?" I ask.

"Nothing." She places her hand protectively over her pocket as if she's worried, I might try to steal it from her.

"You do realize what it is we do, right?"

"Jeadda, I know. Shit girl, let a bitch have a moment," she protests.

Candace walks away, dropping the card at my feet. Don't get me wrong, I don't begrudge my friend a Boo-thang—Lord knows, I'm actively pursuing my own—but a cop? There's just no way to spin that one to make it work. Not now, when we're so close. Oh shit, I just realized what a hypocrite I am. In my defense though, Cofaxx is a 'FORMER' cop, so that doesn't really count.

CHAPTER 17

ODD ALLIANCES

It's been several weeks now, and not a peep from Nu Dinh or Don Diamante. Clearly, the LF12's demise has stirred some reluctance in Gangland. Still, my Siren-ey sense is tingling. It's like I can detect a deep contentious simmering in the streets. Our recent surveillance backs my feelings up, but we still can't get a bead on what the two rival organizations are up to.

It seems that not only have our plans for infiltrating The Family suffered a setback not to mention, we may have inadvertently given the mobsters an unexpected heads-up about us in the person of Maxine. On a breezy Cali night, the Mobsters kidnap her and take her to an abandoned tenement building near the pier, where she is gagged and tied up. Imagine Maxine's face, bruised and bloody, thanks to a harsh slap session—sobbing for mercy as the Don circles.

Don Diamante begins to pour liquor over the helpless escort as he elucidates, "This can be a very unpleasant business. To be successful, you have to be willing to step closer to the edge than anyone else," Diamante explains as if acting out a God Father monologue.

The Don removes the gag from Maxine's mouth. "Please, I have a little girl that needs me. She's only four," Maxine pleads.

"Do you know why I'm so good at what I do?" Maxine does not respond. "I'm so good because I don't see the edge. I've lost a son and a nephew already... and I'm willing to lose everyone in this room if it means I win the war. So, you tell me, why the fuck would I mind ending your worthless junky life just for the hell of it!?" Diamante shoves his fat finger in her face. "Now I'm gonna ask you this one more time. Who are you working for?!" he bellows, frothing at the mouth.

"I swear to you, her name was Jade. She threatened to kill me unless I promised to help... made me call Vick for a date. A black girl with an accent. I swear, her number's right there in my phone..."

Don Diamante wipes some blood from Maxine's lip. "You know what, I believe you." His face drips with sincerity, completely contradictory to his deeds. "I hope you understand, all this, it's not personal for me... just business. Can you find it in your heart to forgive me?"

Maxine nods, Yes.

Don Diamante smiles. "Thank you... and may God have mercy on your soul." He strikes a match and sets Maxine on fire.

She screams like a banshee as she is burned alive.

Israel St. Claire smiles widely at the sight.

The Don tosses the phone to one of his men.

"SOMEBODY GET ME WHO'S RESPONSIBLE FOR THIS... NOW!"

That Monday morning, Israel and two goons march into an office building where they are greeted and escorted, by Yukoshi lackeys, to a penthouse office overlooking China Town.

The Dinh brothers and even more flunkies are also present for this meeting. Quan is seated on a couch while Lanh plays golf on a Wii game system connected to a very large flat-screen TV.

"Well, well, the infamous, Isreal St. Claire—It is a pleasure to finally make your acquaintance. Your reputation for beauty is well deserved. Sit please," Quan offers.

"Thank you, Mr. Dinh."

Lanh misses a putt. "Shit!" he shouts.

"You will have to forgive my brother. Manners were never his strong suit. So, what brings you to China Town?" remarks Quan.

"I have been sent by my employer, Don Diamant'e, to extend an invitation."

Quan is amused by the proposal. "An invitation to what... his funeral?"

"The Don proposes a truce between our organizations. He feels that we should band together to eliminate the ones responsible for these recent assassinations."

Quan is skeptical that the Don isn't responsible for the offenses committed against his father's Yukoshi, including his sister's abduction. "And then?" he asks.

"Then, we will divide San Francisco fairly." It sounds laughable, even to her, but her job is only to deliver the message, not to interpret it.

"No truce!" Lanh cries as he jumps over the couch and plops down next to his brother. He is struck by Israel's beauty. "Damn, oh Hi" he acknowledges.

Quan rolls his eyes and ignores his idiot sibling. He clarifies, "So let me get this straight, you want us to meet the Don for peace talks? And why should we do that? In case you haven't noticed... we're winning this War."

"Yeah, you might want to fill out an application with Dinh Corp, Honey. I'm sure I have a few positions I can put you in," Lanh agrees.

Isreal flashes a snide smile. "Respectfully speaking, it would be unwise to underestimate The Family. The Don recognizes there's no more need for bloodshed, but he **WILL** do what is necessary."

"And do you think we won't?" Lanh retorts.

"I think that you're both intelligent businessmen, who want to protect the things and people that are important to you."

Quan is openly impressed by her. "Okay, we will meet... someplace neutral."

"Fantastic, the Don will be pleased." Her mission accomplished; Isreal stands to leave. "I will be contacting you to discuss further arrangements. Thank you, gentlemen." Israel allows herself to give Quan a warmer, departing handshake.

The messengers leave and Lanh is contemptuous. "You're not seriously considering this so-called truce, are you? We should have fucked that little bitch to death and tossed her on the Don's doorstep!" he scoffs.

"Easy little Brother... I'm no fool. There won't be any truce—but can you think of a better way to get the Don out in the open?" The two brothers smile deviously at each other.

On the way back to her limo, Israel updates the Don on her cell concluding with her account of the meeting's positive ending.

Her driver remarks: "This is crazy. Why would the Don want a truce with the Yukoshi?"

"Trust me, there will be no truce," Israel assures him. "Those arrogant little boys won't leave that meeting alive."

CLICK!!! The high-resolution camera snaps another digital image.

Unknown to either Israel or the Dinh brothers, Deseree has managed to film and record the entire meeting using carefully placed surveillance gear. Suddenly, the Sirens have a new mission!

Cofaxx quickly devises a plan that will allow us to kill these two very large birds with one Mother Fucker of a large stone. Only I seem to notice how overly cautious he is in developing his strategy. He micromanages every possible step to eliminate any improvising. This time, it's like he's preparing to send his adolescent daughters off to finishing school.

We prepare ourselves for the physical demands such a large-scale battle will entail. Madison wires the location where the two organizations plan to meet. She also captures the cell phone conversations of organization members. We are not surprised to learn that both factions are still planning to double-cross and massacre one another.

The talks are scheduled for Labor Day, at a closed office building that used to house the Globa-Con Corporation. So most of the San Fran police force will be busy running crowd control.

While sparring with Candace, I notice her distraction. I believe, "What the hell do you think you're doing?" were my exact words. She explains that she has somewhere she needs to be and asks me to cover for her. Yes, we are a week away from the fight of our lives but, that's part of the reason I agree. Unlike me, Candace has loose ends that need tying. At that moment, I realize there's so much I have yet to experience.

"Cofaxx!" I holler. He's at the command center with Madison.

"Yes, Jeadda?" The words send warm vibrations through me.

"I was just thinking... If we're supposed to be in for such a tough fight, does it really make sense for us to be training around the clock? Don't you think we should take a break and get some rest?"

The Sirens take five to see how this'll play out. "Oh, so now yuh runnin' tings? Well, I say wi nuh dun yet, so dir!" Dalia gripes.

But the others are with me. "Jeadda's right, I can barely feel my legs," Ryan gripes.

Cofaxx eyes me curiously. "Fine, we'll meet back here in two days," he concedes.

The ladies cheer—all except Dalia, whose scowl catches the side of my head. No worries—Candace's look of appreciation is reward enough for me. We head our separate ways but Dalia lingers, studying the way Cofaxx and I interact.

Little did I know, that the personal business Candace just had to blow off training for, was nothing more than a booty call with that cheesy Detective. Not to say that's all that happened, I'm sure he at least took her to dinner but Sex was definitely how the night ended, and furthermore—that Bitch tricked me! Well, it better have been worth it, cuz I ain't letting that sneaky little heffa out of my sight again, til this mission is in the books—and that's a promise!

Later, when Candace gives me the blow-by-blow, I realize how familiar her story is to my own forbidden tryst. I can't even be mad at the girl as she tells me how they collapsed in each other's arms—that she rested her head on his chest and held him tightly, afraid to let go.

I don't kiss and tell in return—Oh, I want to, but the knowledge of mine and Cofaxx's affair would totally destroy everything we've accomplished here. I can tell you now, only in retrospect, that after everyone left that night, Cofaxx and I made love all over his office.

Lying there, with him playing in my sweat-curled baby hair, I asked the million-dollar question that'd been weighing on my mind. "You know why I'm here. Why I want Dunlock, so badly..." Let's not kid ourselves, my psychological scars are almost as visible as the physical ones fighting criminals had created. "But you—he's your brother! I find it hard to swallow, that this is all just about some pursuit of law and order."

Cofaxx reluctantly tells me how, as children, he and Dunlock were inseparable. The best of brothers and friends, they carved their initials into a tree near their home, along with the word 'Brothers.' His voice quivers, as he explains how Dunlock's subsequent kidnapping gave him nightmares for the better part of his young adult life. Cofaxx cursed himself for not doing more to save his sibling.

That all ended the day he met Lauren. He could finally rest with an easy heart and he knew the emotional peace he felt was due to her. On the day he graduated—better yet survived Marine boot camp, Cofaxx received the call he had secretly been hoping for. The voice from so long ago was deeper but still recognizable—it was Di Tiaay, calling to congratulate his long-lost baby brother. The young men made plans to reunite and Cofaxx had never been happier in his life.

Cofaxx flew back to Angola where he was greeted by his brother who was also in uniform. However, to Luther's dismay, it was the uniform of a rebel contra. As Dunlock took him on a 'grand tour' of their war-torn country, Cofaxx discovered his bro had made quite a name for himself. Dunlock asked his younger sibling to stay and rule by his side in the criminal empire he'd built. It would be a life of tyranny and terrorism of the kind that had made them orphans as children.

Cofaxx couldn't convince the power-mad Dunlock to abandon his twisted plans. In the end, he was forced to flee back to America, barely escaping from his enraged brother with his own life intact.

Cofaxx and his new bride relocated far away from his former Marine base, but Dunlock managed to track them down. He felt betrayed by the brother whose life he'd saved as a child. Now Cofaxx owed him that life and he would pay for it one way or another.

So, Dunlock took the one thing Cofaxx cherished —he stole the lives of the man's one true love, Lauren, and their unborn child. Cofaxx found her beaten and strangled to death. Written next to her body, in blood, was the word… 'Brothers.'

"Oh my God, I am so sorry," I whisper.

"It is the past and I have had my time to mourn. Now, I just want to make sure he can't hurt anyone else," he tells me. He says it, but I don't believe a word—I can't. I've seen him weep devastated tears of guilt and loss. I have grown to know his passion and can imagine the intensity of his love for her.

"You know, Jeadda this whole thing… this mission. I'm afraid, I have pulled you girls into my obsession and put your lives in danger. Dunlock has already stolen so much from me. I couldn't bare it if he hurt you…" See there, his consideration for us is only further proof of his—'WHAT!!! Whoa, hold the hell up, what did he just say!?'

I peel myself off of him. "What are you saying?" I question, reading into his face.

"I think I may have made a mistake... perhaps I should call off this mission."

I can't believe what I'm hearing. "You're backing down now, after all this? You... you can't do this! You can't take this from me! You promised me!" I demand, standing to my feet with nothing more than his T-shirt to cover me.

He tries to rationalize his comment further, but I refuse to listen—the disgust I feel leaves a bitter taste in my mouth. He had just given a list of reasons why Dunlock deserves the fate I have planned for him and I'm not just going to get over what he's done to me or the ones I love. He will pay and that's final!

"No, I don't want to hear it! We are doing this, with or without your help," I yell, before storming out in my nakedness.

What neither of us knew, is that Dalia had been hiding within the facility and watching the whole encounter—must have been pretty entertaining, I imagine.

CHAPTER 18

UNUSUAL SUSPECTS

The next night finds Lanh over in Chinatown, in the middle of a high-stakes Chinese card game, similar to American poker. He sits at a small table with three other Asian gamblers, each staring at his own cards. Lanh downs shot after shot of hard liquor and smokes like a chimney. "I raise you five-hundred dollars," Lanh announces to his cronies. The mood becomes tense while the men study each other for tells.

One of them places his cards face down proclaiming, "I'm out. It's not worth it."

Another man follows suit. "Me, too."

"You should be ashamed to call yourselves men!" Lanh sneers.

One challenger remains—a nearly toothless old retch. "What about you, old man… do you have anything left to wager? Maybe that tooth," Lanh jokes gesturing towards the last tooth the man has in his rotted mouth. For an answer, the man removes an ancient ruby ring from his shirt pocket and slides it over to Lanh. He inspects it for a moment. To his way of thinking, it's not something an old fart deserves to have. It's more befitting of a young prince—and that's just what Lanh is.

"Alright, fine," he tells the man dropping it in the till.

The old man discards a card into a stack and takes another. Lanh swallows another shot of booze to help him tolerate the time wasted by the relic examining his hand. "Stop wishing for better luck. Play the hand the fates have dealt to you!" Lanh barks.

"I will stay," the old man declares.

Lanh smiles arrogantly. "There's a brave man. I'm almost ashamed to have to do this to you." He lays his cards down on the table in triumph. The dusty old man studies them against what he has in his own hands. He also grins, his lonely greying fossil hanging in his vacant gums for dear life. He slowly lays his cards down and to the shock of everyone around the table, he has won—he's beaten Lanh.

The old man wraps his arms around the pile of money resting between them. Lanh's face morphs into a mask of fury. Suddenly, his foot flies across the table striking the old man in the mouth and knocking out his last tooth. Lanh bashes the dealer and the other two men, as well. He eyes the Bartender who is suddenly frozen in fear. The villain grabs his bottle of alcohol but leaves the money—after all, he's a poor sport, but not a cheat.

Lanh stumbles out of the bar, into the night. He tosses the bottle and teeters down the street until he reaches a candy-apple red Porshe Boxter. The inebriated man drops his keys on the ground as he attempts to open the door and bending over to get them, he fails to notice someone in his passenger's seat. Eventually, he opens the door and tips himself into the driver's seat. Lanh rests his head on the steering wheel with a weary, drunken groan.

An electronic alert reminds him that the door is still open. "Hey, shut your mouth!" he yells at the car. Lanh closes the door, laughs, and fumbles to fit the key in the ignition. Only upon turning it does he happen to glance over at the figure seated next to him. Lanh's eyes bug wide open in terror: His passenger is the scorched body of Maxine!

KABLAAM!

Lanh's Ferrari explodes in a huge ball of fire, shooting the doors off their hinges and lifting the frame into the air. Asian Bar B Que Anyone?

I know what you're thinking: 'Why would The Family waste Nu Dinh's son if they were intent on negotiating a truce with the Yukoshi?' The answer is simple—They didn't, we did... really, Dalia did. She confessed later that she'd been tracking Maxine ever since she murdered Victor and after she located her body—nothing more than turkey jerky. Dalia transported the corpse to Lanh's car. In my opinion, her whole story was pretty God damn twisted—and her devilish laugh didn't help things.

That night, Candace stops by the club to retrieve a charm necklace from her locker. It was a teen-aged birthday gift from me that we've worn since back in the day—a good luck charm of sorts and we would need all the luck we could summon.

She gets a call from an unknown number, and being Candace, she answers. "Hello?" No response back so again, being Candace, "If you can hear me, I can't hear you. Call me back, okay—Bye?" she hangs up and leaves. What my little friend doesn't know is that Giovanni is on the other end and he's tracked her location. Candace drives away from Eye Candy, narrowly missing an entire caravan of black vehicles that arrives at the club, mere seconds later.

Inside, Sir Mont'e is busy hob-nobbing with one of the regulars at the bar. A flood of Italian men in black suits storm into the Main Room.

"Now what is this? Aww, hold up... this shit don't look right," Sir mutters.

The men pull out weapons and open fire on patrons. The bouncers instinctively return 'hot led', along with Sir Monte. "You mother fuckers think you just gone come up in my God damn club, shooting... this club right here, nigga... this club right here?"

Sir Mont'e runs out of ammo and dives behind the bar. Quickly re-emerging with a sawed-off shotgun, he blasts away. The surviving bandits beat a quick retreat.

News of the hit permeates every major channel, serving as one more reason for me and my fellow Sirens to destroy these gangs. We strenuously prepare for the task ahead, vowing to ourselves and each other that the culprits will pay with their lives.

By this time, detectives Carone and Bates are on their way back to the Hub. Sonny studies photos that were frame-grabbed from the video footage found at the Four Seasons.

"What am I supposed to be looking at, here?" he asks his focused partner.

"It's not what you see; it's what you don't see," Arturo exclaims. "Anytime someone visited or left that suite, Victor was at the door. But in the last few photos one woman arrives, a different girl leaves the next morning—and guess who's not playing Doorman when she exits?"

"Yeah, a working girl with a wig, so what?" Sonny probes.

Realizing his partner hasn't caught on, Detective Carone offers: "I studied that tape for hours. There's no way Giovanni could have committed that murder. There just wasn't enough time—He was already dead."

"So, you think Victor got offed by a call-girl? That's going to be a hard one to sell to the Captain. And who is this Mighty Morphin Ninja Hooker supposed to be, anyway?" Sonny indulges.

"I'm not sure, but I've got a hunch." Arturo puts his foot down on the accelerator, speeding through traffic.

Sonny stares at him oddly. "Well, at least tell me where we're going?" he lobbies.

"You'll see."

"You know what... you have communication issues.
You need to work on that," Sonny suggests.

"Mmm hmm," Arturo offers, as the men proceed in hot pursuit of his premonition.

Over at Nu Dinh's mansion, Quan and his father watch a news report about Lanh's car bomb explosion and death. Nu Dinh cups his face in his hands and sobs for his youngest son—he has to wager that his lifestyle has cost him dearly this day.

Just then, Quan receives a call from Israel. "How dare you call this house!" he snarls.

"I'm calling on behalf of Don Diamante. He sends his deepest condolences for your loss and wants to assure you that The Family was not involved," she reports. "We have discovered a mutual enemy Mr. Dinh... and we have proof." The news, even if it were believable can't possibly be assessed in Quan's current mental state.

"Tell me who?" Quan demands.

"All will be explained at the meeting... you will still be there, correct?"

"I will be there," Quan growls. He slams the phone down.

"Father, forgive me. I swear to you on my life that I will find who did this and avenge my brother," he vows. Quan puts his hand on his mourning father's shoulder. "Where is Mao Lei?" he asks.

"I sent her away with Daygo. I trust he will protect her with **_his_** life," Nu Dinh replies still unaware of the couple's arrangement.

"Yes, father."

At that very moment, the Detectives pull up outside of The Hub.

"So let me get this straight… you wanna raid the self-defense class… for real?" Sonny poses the ludicrous notion, with a sarcastic side-eye. Of course, he can't divulge the true reason for his hesitance.

"Think about it, Cofaxx has as big a grudge against these criminals as we do—especially Dunlock. He's been living with guilt for years. It was only a matter of time before something like that would eat through him," Arturo asserts.

Arturo buzzes the com but receives no answer. "Looks like nobody's home." He stares fixedly at the intricate keypad on it.

"Take it as a sign. Maybe God doesn't want us to lose our jobs today," Sonny suggests.

"Give me a sec." Arturo enters a code into the system. An automated voice denies access. He tries several more times.

"It's going to take you all year to hack a system like this," Sonny cautions.

Then Arturo tries one last time, entering the name Cofaxx had chosen for his unborn son, Omari. Access is granted. I'd have given anything to see the look on their faces when they step inside.

The HUB is empty!

You see, after their previous visit, Cofaxx had decided we should find a more secluded location. We moved our operation into a new facility, which we call the HIVE.

"Tell me something partner, what kind of person shuts down their entire operation less than a week after getting visited by the Police? A guilty one!" Arturo says as they depart.

As for me, I've been thinking hard about what Cofaxx revealed to me. I wonder what's going to happen once Dunlock is dead. Will my nightmares just end, or will they be replaced with new nightmares about the lives I've taken? I wonder if there is such a thing as redemption for someone like me.

With that on my mind, it's no coincidence, I find myself sitting in a confessional booth at a Catholic church, seeking answers from a God I'm not even sure I believe in.

A kind voice greets me. "Welcome, my child," it says. I don't know whether I expect to hear, the voice of God or what, but I'm more nervous than I've been in quite some time.

"I'm not sure how to do this. Not even sure if I'm Catholic. I just wanted to ask God for forgiveness," I murmur to the priest.

"Certainly, you have come to the right place. There is no wrong way to confess... just be honest and speak freely as if you were talking to your father," he suggests. The comment catches me off guard and I imagine my father's response to what I've been doing. I wonder if God's love is as unconditional as my fathers was.

"I just want God to know that I'm not a bad person, in spite of the things I've done. I've lived most of my life in fear... scared of all the bad people out there. Now, I've found a way to fight back. But I worry... I may have become one of the bad people I used to be so afraid of. I need some kind of a sign," I admit.

"Fear not my child, for the Lord knows our hearts and is watching over us even in the most troubling of times. If we only trust in him, he will provide the answers we seek."

"Even to a sinner," I ask.

"Especially to a sinner," he confirms.

I want to believe that I can be forgiven by some all-knowing, all-seeing, all-powerful deity, but the truth is that His forgiveness isn't my primary concern. I really don't know how I will forgive myself.

The Priest continues. "Now, tell me, child, what do you want to confess?" Sorry man, by then I'm long gone.

Sure, it might help to know if forgiveness is possible, but I also have a mission and can't be second-guessing myself out there. I figure if God digs me, he'll understand I don't have a choice in all of this anymore.

CHAPTER 19

NO TRUCE

The Labor Day Parade marches down city streets congested with cheering on-lookers. The Yukoshi park in the middle level of Globa-Con's garage in a fleet of pearl white automobiles. Moments later, per their agreement, The Family in black sedans pull into the level above them.

Deseree secures a sniper position facing the garage and watches them through her rifle scope. From there, she can see everything. "They're in," she confirms over her com.

Madison and the still healing Ryan, monitor both organizations on a video feed streaming from video equipment hidden within the building. From their position parked in a nearby windowless van, they relay crucial tactical details to us.

Jazmine, Candace, Dalia, and I, have already infiltrated the building. We silently move through it, nabbing optimal strike positions. Globa-Con appears to be either undergoing radical renovation or preparing for demolition. Scaffolding and other building materials are scattered everywhere, making for dangerous navigation and plenty of opportunities to injure oneself. I curse under my breath when I snag my arm on a loose nail. "Dammit, that's gonna require a tetanus shot."

The two groups file into the building's spacious lobby. They remind me of opposing chess pieces—The Family adorned in all Black, and the Yukoshi in White. Don Diamante takes the lead, stepping forward. "Mister Dinh, thank you for agreeing to meet with me today. I know our two organizations have somewhat of a checkered past, but despite that, I'm optimistic about the future."

Their respective bodyguards engage one another in a tense stare down, each side waiting for the 'GO AHEAD.'

"You know we aren't so different, you and me. We're just a couple of guys, bound by pride and tradition—trying to protect it at all costs. So, here's what I propose we do... a truce, mutually beneficial for the both of us."

Quan, by his father's side, glares at the Don, disgusted. "And just what would be the terms of such an agreement?" Nu inquires.

The Don's mouth curls into a grin. "Hey, now we're talking. I'm thinking, I keep Family business away from Chinatown and you guys stay out of my territory, see... and hey, on top of that, we muscle out anyone who gets in the way. Split the city right down the middle, huh?" the Don recommends, smiling triumphantly.

Nu Dinh reflects on the proposal. "And when you decide that it is no longer in your best interest to share control of the city? What happens then?"

"Hey, look, I don't know what the future holds any more than you do. All I'm saying is, right now we have an opportunity to seize control, so why not do it? What do you say, huh... we got a deal?" Don Diamant'e extends his hand to Nu Dinh.

Dinh looks at the Don's hand and shakes his head. "Mr. Diamante, while you are correct about this being an unprecedented opportunity, your lust for money and power will never be satisfied and I will never be able to trust you. I am afraid I must decline your offer... for a deal with a dishonorable man is no deal at all," he reasons.

The Don's face turns beet red with anger. "Oh, is that right? So, I come here to talk to you, out of respect, like two gentlemen... and this is how you repay me? You spit on my generosity... huh," he bellows. The Don pulls his weapon and points it at Dinh's head igniting an all-around drawdown.

At that very moment, on the second level, a patrolling Yukoshi henchman finds Candace. He pads over to the desk she's hiding behind and surprises her. Candace makes quick work of him, but her finishing blow sends him over the banister, down into the lobby. The soldier lands between the two groups, his neck broken.

GREENLIGHT!!!

So, yeah, this is where shit gets TURNED ALL THE WAY UP! Don Diamante shoots Nu Dinh in the head. Quan retaliates by blowing off the Don's facial features with a Glock 30.

The two opposing forces scatter throughout the building, dispersing each other in a Wild West-style gunfight. Of course, we join in the fray, fighting valiantly as gangsters swarm like killer bees from all directions. Despite our planning, their numbers are choking and we are divided— cut off from one another and each forced to pit for themselves.

After dropping several soldiers, Jazmine finally escapes to the section of the garage where The Family has parked their cars. She pauses to examine the impressive vehicles before focusing her gaze on an old-school black muscle car. Jazzy grins. "Oh... come to Momma."

Back in the building, Quan Dinh is busy shooting mobsters when he is hit once in the chest by Giovanni. Quan drops his gun and flees down an empty hall. Giovanni blasts another enemy, then follows Quan. The blood trail left by Dinh's oldest son leads to a closed door. Giovanni cautiously enters the room, pistol raised.

He stalks slowly through the dark space in search of a now-hidden warrior. Without warning, a hook-ended rope snags his leg, yanking him to the floor. Quan attacks and the two men brawl. Furious strikes are tossed back and forth until Quan wraps the rope around Giovanni's neck, choking him.

Giovanni pushes his finger into the wound on Quan's chest causing the man to holler out in pain. He head-butts Giovanni and forces him through a window. Shattered glass rains down upon the mobster as he's hanged—dangling from the building like a cryptic tea bag.

Quan stumbles towards the door but the bullet in his chest has finally taken its toll. He reaches back and discovers that his jacket is soaked with blood from the fatal shot. He crumples—already dead before he hits the floor.

Candace enters the parking structure, on a lower level, where two Yukoshi goons on motorcycles spot her and race towards her. She dodges one of them and whip-kicks the other off of his bike.

The man she dodged revs his engine preparing again to charge. Candace settles into an attack stance with one hand in the air. She snaps her fingers just as a bullet from Deseree's rifle blows him off the bike.

"Not today, buddy," Deseree declares from her firing block. Candace salutes her teammate before helping herself to the man's helmet and bike.

Back inside, Dalia runs through the halls shooting armed Family henchmen, until she uses up her ammo. She drops her guns and heads for the garage where she's eventually dead-ended by a brick wall.

Now, her back literally against the wall, Dalia pulls out a sword and prepares to face them but there's one problem—***they*** haven't run out of bullets! The men laugh as they approach her, reloading their weapons.

Suddenly, the sound of screeching tires echoes through the garage!

As if from nowhere, Jazmine drifts down a spiral ramp in the black hot rod she was eyeing and fires at the men—they scatter. Dalia jumps into the car and grabs a loaded M-16. She blasts away while Jazmine speeds down another ramp.

Back inside, I run through a blurred maze of empty cubicles, shooting at members of The Family and the Yukoshi—all of whom seem more interested in shooting at me than each other. I'm able to dip into a restroom where I take a sec to catch my breath and figure out an escape route. The only thing I find is an air conditioning shaft above the stalls.

Three mercenaries stand outside the door. They shoot through the wall like cowards before carefully entering only to notice that the ventilation grate has been opened. Peering up at the ceiling, listening for movements that will alert them to my position, they work their way back toward the exit.

Their collective eyes bug as they find me, perched above the door, where I have been the entire time. "Gotcha," I confirm, popping all three men in the head—silly, I know, but I've always wanted to use one of those bad-ass Charles Bronson – Death Wish, catchphrases. Don't judge me.

I dismount and crack the door to check my evacuation options. I'm trapped between more armed soldiers and a wall of glass—my choice is simple. I charge toward the window wall as the gunmen fire behind me. They shoot out the glass just enough for me and I dive through, narrowly grabbing onto the scaffolding situated outside. All in all, I suffer a rough landing but miraculously sustain only a few minor cuts and a slightly twisted ankle. I'm certain it's better than the alternative.

Using the ropes from the platform, I swing to a lower level and I too enter the parking garage. As I limp passed cement pillars, I am halted in my tracks by the sound of screeching motorcycle tires. I dive behind some building materials just in time to see a motorbike pull to a stop, facing away from me—big mistake! I aim for the rider's helmet ready to one-shot one-kill his ass. Just as I'm about to squeeze the trigger, the cyclist removes the headgear. It's Candace! I realize, I nearly killed my best friend. "Candace! Girl, I almost shot you... whose bike is this?" I ask, still a bit stunned by my good fortune—and hers.

"You mean like, his name?" Candace gives a puzzled shrug.

Yukoshi soldiers race into the garage and I jump on the bike behind Candace. We speed away—nearly clipping the car Jazzy and Dalia are in, as we all explode out onto the street.

Several cars emerge from the structure and give chase through the busy San Francisco shopping district. Candace skillfully avoids traffic while I shoot at our followers. Dalia hangs out the passenger-side door of the car and caps one of the drivers. He crashes into a row of parked vehicles.

Forced to break route when we're met by parade traffic, we speed down a side street with one car in fast pursuit. We whiz through busy intersections as I remove the shotgun strapped to Candace's back. I wrap my legs around her waist, and lay back taking careful aim. I shoot the latch off the hood of the car and it flies up, blinding the driver as the car skids to a stop.

BAAAM!!! The car is suddenly crushed by an oncoming Big-Rig.

Headed for the Hive, Candace and I cut down another street, which funnels onto the Golden Gate Bridge.

Meanwhile, just behind us, Jazmine's hydro-boosted vehicle darts away from Yukoshi, Family, and the police that have joined in this chase. She speeds past an 18-wheeled truck hauling a flatbed trailer. Dalia rolls down the passenger side window and shoots out the driver's side tires jackknifing the truck and blocking all pursuers—allowing them to get away.

Candace and I arrive back at the HIVE first, or so we think. We immediately notice the place is a combat zone—littered with bullet holes. Bodies of mop-top soldiers lay in bloody pools all around the gym.

"What happened here," Candace cries.

"Shhh, they might still be here," I whisper.

We move through the building with our weapons pointed at everything. I notice that the door to Cofaxx's office is closed and the bloodstained handprints on it hit my heart with a burning grief.

Inside the disheveled room, the horrifying scene cuts deep like a pot of homicidal Gumbo. Blood, bullet casings, and body chunks are strewn everywhere. Scrap lies on the floor, expired from a gunshot blast to the chest. Candace folds up against the wall like, her bones have disintegrated.

Moments later, the rest of the team bursts into the office. Ryan crumbles beside her lifeless comrade. She sobs inconsolably as the rest of us try not to lose our shit to the soundtrack of her muffled screams. His finger remains wrapped loosely around the trigger of the Astra A-60 still held in his custom waist-holster mechanism. Scrap's heroic last stand.

Suddenly, a grouchy old laugh blusters from behind Cofaxx's desk, nearly scaring the piss right out of me. We leap into action and quickly locate a wounded T.R.A.P. soldier leaning against the back wall. "How precious," the dying man chuckles. Dalia puts her gun to his head.

"Dalia, wait! He may know something," I shout.

"Where have they taken Cofaxx?"

"Fuck you!" the smelly 'Dread-head' coughs. Dalia hits him in the face but he laughs again. "Stupid gyal... meh hab already made a pact wit dih debil. Yah canno kill meh, Bitch!"

Dalia smiles, having just received her Tik-Tok challenge.

"Wanna bet," she quizzes.

The man realizes his mistake just before Dalia fires a bullet into his dome, disproving his theory.

"What are we supposed to do now?" Deseree whimpers.

"I have an idea," Madison declares, rushing out of the office. As the rest of us, combined have nowhere near her I.Q. we have no choice but to follow our little genius. Much of the equipment has sustained damage, but Madison is able to pull up a tracking beacon program.

Cofaxx insisted we all be chipped—part of his 'No Man Left Behind' policy; who would have thought we'd be using it to locate him.

"Okay, Cofaxx is being transported Westbound, back through the city" Madison informs. "That's him, see." She points to a blip on her console screen. "Looks like they've got about a thirty-to-thirty-five-minute lead on us."

"Do you have any idea where they're taking him?" I probe.

"Well, it's hard to be exact, but if I were looking for a hideout, I'd probably head here." Madison points out a large piece of land with a structure on it, just ahead of Cofaxx's convoy. "My scans indicate an elaborate network of tunnels beneath it... It might be some sort of bunker."

Jazmine joins us, carrying a small bag of weapons.

"This is all that's left," she reports.

Ryan shuffles through the bag. "What're we supposed to do with this, stick up a girl-scout troop?"

I glare at the blinking beacon and the answer is very clear to me. "We finish what we started... Cofaxx would do it for any of us!" The ladies agree—even Dalia.

We set out to attack the compound.

On the drive over, all of us are plagued by pretty much the same nagging idea: If they can take Cofaxx, what chance do we have? I try to comfort myself by imagining a scenario in which he allowed himself to be captured so we could track him to Dunlock's hideout. It doesn't work, but I have to fake it for all of our sakes.

As the impromptu leader of these Estrogen-fueled Assassins, it's my duty to protect them—even from the notion of defeat. Imagine that—me of all people, a team player. I can hardly fathom it myself.

CHAPTER 20

FINAL RESOLUTION

Cofaxx is bound inside Dunlock's office. Blakk spent a generous moment beating him and now stands over the battered man while Dunlock circles them, doing the whole, 'How could you betray your family?' number.

Israel watches the show. Turns out, she was a spy for Dunlock all along. What a sneaky little hoe... I guess, she belongs to the streets.

"Little brother, you have caused me a great deal of trouble," Dunlock hums. "Tell me, what will it take for you to let the past go?"

Cofaxx struggles to lift his bloody head. "I will let it go... when you are behind bars." This response wins him a strike in the face from Blakk.

"Mudda Focka!" Blakk grunts.

Dunlock continues to circle. "So, you want me in chains? How ironic, since I've already spent half of my life in prison for you. If it hadn't been for my sacrifice, you never would have survived our childhood." He frowns, letting his rage build. "The life you live should be in servitude to me! YOU OWE ME!"

"You took my heart from me, any debt I owed you is paid in full," Cofaxx replies.

Dunlock kicks his brother in the stomach. "Get him out of my sight!" he yells.

Blakk drags Cofaxx away.

Meanwhile, Arturo and Sonny have staked out near the T.R.A.P. compound in the unmarked car after discovering the vacant Hub. They are now working off Freddy's intel. For them, everything has been rather quiet, barring a few insignificant comings and goings.

Sonny's patience is running thin. "Man, I'm tired of all this waiting around. Why don't we just bust through the gate, and take the damn place?"

Arturo is a big protocol nerd. He's been doing this long enough to have experienced the sting of rushing in all half-cocked. "Don't be such a rookie," he instructs.

"I thought Freddy said this is the place? What else do we need?"

"**_We_**, don't need anything. But **_We_** don't matter. All the **_Prosecutor_** will need is Probable Cause. So, for now, **_We_** wait."

The Sirens, however, are burdened by no such obligations to the law. Our armored van speeds right passed the cops crashing through the security gate.

"Is that probable enough for you?" Sonny asks.

"Works for me." Arturo puts in a call to alert the Scorpions that it is 'go time.'

Inside of Dunlock's office, our villains watch the commotion on a surveillance monitor as the van circles the building, dispersing cover fire in all directions. Dunlock's goons scatter, taking positions to defend the compound. He speaks into an intercom and his commands thunder throughout the area, like the voice of a Greek God. "I want dem dead!"

The van finally stops and is riddled with bullets. Once the smoke clears, the guards approach the disabled vehicle—now dead in the dirt. Cautiously opening the rear doors reveals it's empty—not to mention, rigged to blow, playing "No woman; No cry." The van explodes sending baddies flying across the property.

Madison is inside another vehicle, controlling the dupe-van by remote. "Alright, ladies, they're going to be on you soon," she alerts.

Where are we? We're navigating our way through escape tunnels strategically built under the compound. Dunlock, in his unmitigated arrogance never figured they would be traversed. Men, they never pay attention to the little things.

We reach a ladder that leads above ground. Up we climb; emerging from a manhole in one of the compound's four garages and find ourselves ass deep in a mother-load of automotive power and extravagance—it's a wonder Jazzy doesn't bust a nut at the sight of all of those exotic cars.

As team captain, I give the signal to split the group into smaller units. Team 1 is comprised of Dalia and Candace. They head through a door that takes them to a parlor in Dunlock's luxurious mansion living quarters. Team 2—that's Deseree and me, take a service elevator to the kitchen. Team 3, made up of Jazmine and Ryan, will run support for us, defending the second-floor stairway.

The guards rush into Dunlock's mansion armed to the teeth in search of intruders but I'm sure they don't expect us. I doubt that'll prevent them from capping our asses, but it will certainly make for some odd glares.

While all this is going on, Arturo and Sonny have driven through the smashed gate, into the compound. By the time they reach the entrance, the mansion echoes with so many competing gun pops and muzzle flashes that it's difficult to determine which way to duck.

Dalia and Candace are engaged in an intense encounter in the parlor and have taken positions behind the bar. They are being fired upon by soldiers, including Reese and Israel. Dalia shoots one of the gunmen who sprays wildly as he falls, killing another. Candace eventually runs out of ammo. "Improvise!" Dalia shouts.

Candace searches through drawers on the bar and finds one of them is full of knives. She dumps the contents out on the floor and begins to hurl blades at the shooters. Candace catches one man in the throat and another in his shooting hand. The man drops his gun and Dalia gleefully blasts him.

Candace cycles through all the knives but several shooters still remain. "I've got an idea... cover me," she instructs Dalia. Candace begins to throw full bottles of alcohol at the shooters, drenching the floors around them. The men laugh at her feeble attempts to bottle-bash them to death.

"Dem all outta fiyah," one of them taunts.

Candace lights up a piece of cloth she's stuffed inside the neck of her last bottle. "You couldn't be more wrong," she murmurs flinging her Molotov Cocktail over the bar. It explodes and the alcohol-covered floors are quickly engulfed in flames.

Like an uncaged cat-woman, Candace jumps through the flames, attacking Reese with solid strikes to his ugly mug. "Oh, di bumboclot Yankee gyal waan box meh? Aright", Reese accepts. He swings wildly at Candace, who ducks his attempts and counters with her own.

Reese grabs the tiny woman in a bear-hug but she knees his groin parts collapsing the huge man on top of her. With that Candace finally gets the chance to use her scissor kick, wrapping her legs around his neck, and squeezing while he struggles to break free. Candace is treated to the satisfying snap of his larynx between her toned thighs. Reese goes limp.

Israel occupies Dalia in a separate but equally brutal fight—smacking and tossing one another around savagely. Israel eventually gets the drop on our teammate knocking Dalia unconscious. Just as she prepares to deliver a fatal blow Candace tackles her. They wrestle on the ground and Israel takes a straddle position, choking her. Candace breaks her hold and they separate on the floor, panting eye to eye. Each woman spots a weapon and they dive in opposite directions for them—spin and unload their guns at point-blank range.

Dalia is awakened by the sound of close fire only to find both Israel and Candace lying on the floor—mortally wounded. Israel quickly expires. Dalia holds Candace and yells into her headset for help. "Help, meh need help here, please!" Her voice breaks so we know it's bad.

Deseree and I catch the call as we sneak through a downstairs hallway at the opposite end of the house. Just then, a team of gunmen runs past us. Deseree grabs the last man, plunging a knife into his chest. I shoot the other two in the back. Dalia's frantic S.O.S calls eventually lead us to the parlor.

We finally arrive, just in time to find Dalia cradling Candace's head and vowing that things would be alright. My little Sis is fading fast. I could have been hit by a truck and not have buckled the way I do at her lying there. It's my fault and I know it immediately. I've taken the only person in this world I really care about—no conditions, and brought her to this. It's as if I've pulled the trigger, again. I beg the universe to let me trade places with her. But there is no such refuge for me—no such escape.

"No, no, no! Get away from her," I hear someone scream hysterically—Is that me? I take Candace from Dalia and wrap her in my arms. Dalia respectfully backs away to give me some grieving room.

Candace opens her eyes, slightly. "Hey, Jea? Did we win?" she asks.

I don't have the heart to tell her the truth. "Yes, mami, we won." Some best friend, I am.

"Good, cuz I'm tired," she admits, sending tears gushing from my eyes.

"It's okay, babe. It's over now," I assure her, and Candace smiles.

"I told you we'd win, Jea," she reminds me.

My body is so stiff trying to comfort her that, all I can do is nod. And with that, my CandaNce closes her eyes and peacefully slips away from me. I'm filled with a rage so intense; that it renders me temporarily psychotic. Everything and everyone must pay!

Deseree can't even bring herself to look at Candace; she just sobs.

For once, Dalia and I are in the same place. She grabs two guns and storms out of the parlor, mowing down a group of T.R.A.P. guards on the way. She blasts her way to Jazmine and Ryan who continue to engage guards coming up the stairs. Together, the trio are a fire-breathing dragon, spitting deadly flames down on Dunlock's men.

I quickly convince myself that the best way I can honor Candace is by winning this war. I am forced to leave her with Deseree and resume my search for Dunlock. Yes, I have to end this the only way I know how—I have to end **him!** My head is so crowded with these thoughts, I'm not even sure if I've already passed the room I need to find. Somehow, I end up in the Master bedroom.

There, I find a passageway near the bed and follow it down a hidden hall, into an office. That's where I find him. He sits behind his desk, not a care in the world. "Dunlock," I roar!

I aim my gun at his chest, knowing a head wound would be too quick; too easy. 'No, this will not be quick—this will be decidedly uneasy.' I want him to suffer!

"Ah, a little girl, with a big gun," his quiet laughter is full of menace.

"Where is Cofaxx?"

"Somewhere safe… but we have plenty of time to discuss him. Come now; let us speak of other things." He lights a cigar and begins to puff. I want to shoot it out of his smug mouth, but at this angle, my bullet would split his fat bald head in two.

"I ain't got nothing to say to you, Mother Fucker!"

"American women… so rude. So, does the rude little girl have a name?" he asks. I blink, uncomprehending. He doesn't even know who I am or why I'm here. Imagine it, to have killed or hurt so many people you have no clue who your enemies are anymore.

I can't kill him without first letting him know exactly why he must die and who it is taking his life. "My name is Jeadda Tibbadaux, and my parents were Ostro and Adrianne Tibbadaux. They were all I had... and you took them from me!"

"Oh, meh sih. Suh, dis iz far revenge? Yuh fight far dih loss un yuh famally. Dat iz honorable. Iz also very naïve. So, tell meh dis, little girl, if you kill me, what iz ih dat yuh gain?"

Dunlock is too warm to the subject—seemingly proud of his handy work. "Will yuh fadda return tuh yuh once I an I gone? No, he won. Will yo mudda magically appear hir befoe us? Yuh hab ris yuh life an dih lies of dem fren fuh ghos!" The bastard is determined to squeeze every last bit of pain out of this situation and although I know he's just trying to rile me, there's nothing I want more at this moment than to give myself over to the storm brewing inside me.

"When I shoot you, I get to see the look on your face as you realize your titanic ego will be snuffed out forever. You'll be gone and forgotten. A nobody." I'm glad to see that gets to him.

"Ahh, but yuh forget won ting. I hab someting yuh waan, isn't dat right, Brother?" he replies. Right on cue, Blakk appears with Cofaxx in tow—beaten, tied, and gagged.

"Befoe yuh can hab yuh appy eva afta, silly gyal, yuh muss finis dih game," Dunlock advises.

"Duh yuh lub dis man?" Blakk asks, joining in the fun. He employs the same heartless question from years ago; the one that's haunted my sleep for so long. Suddenly, I am a small child again, standing in the living room of my home with Blakk's heavy arm draped over my shoulders.

I keep the gun directed at Dunlock.

"Duh... yuh... Lub... dis man?" he repeats. Unfortunately for this, asshole, I'm no longer a child, and contrary to what his boss said—I don't just have a BIG gun. I have two!

I split Blakk between the eyes using the pistol I have holstered on my hip—Scrap's prototype invention. I relish Blakk's last look of surprise. "Yes, I do love him," I affirm.

Blakk falls to the floor in a heavy heap and I take a bead on Dunlock with both pistols.

Time freezes...

At that very moment, Dalia, Jazmine, and Ryan battle another group of soldiers near the stairs.

The Detectives have breached and made their way to the second floor. The partners' take the path leading them to the parlor, where they find Deseree, still guarding Candace's body. "Freeze," they command. She stands, aiming her gun, all the while wondering if she can cross that line. I mean vicious killers was one thing, but vicious killers with badges, a whole other story.

Sonny sees the woman Deseree is protecting and lowers his weapon slowly approaching. He drops to one knee gathering Candace into his arms. "Hey, what are you doing... get away from her!" Deseree demands.

Deseree, by this point, is dumb-faced and has no choice but to relinquish her defense. Of course, she had no clue about Candace's little cop-fling. She and Arturo continue to point their guns toward one another.

"Now, look, it doesn't have to end like this, alright? I can help you. Let me help you. Easy, now... easy." Deseree slowly lowers her gun. Sure, she's logged a pretty decent body count but she's no cop killer. She holsters her weapon.

Arturo enlists Deseree to assist him in finding the others and they leave Sonny cradling his lover on the floor. The two of them navigate the halls eventually entering the Master Bedroom where they overhear my discussion with Dunlock. "Wait here," Arturo instructs Deseree. She obeys, but as soon as he's out of sight she runs off to find the others.

Arturo makes his way toward the office, gun drawn. He intervenes when he sees me about to kill Dunlock.

"Jeadda wait!" I instinctively aim one of my pistols at Arturo's head. "Hey look, you can trust me. I'm putting away my gun." Indeed, he holsters his weapon and slowly walks toward me, hands raised.

I'm not a cop killer either, but at this point, my mind is fogged by murderous desire. Friend and Foe—it just doesn't register. All I see is a person edging uncomfortably close and trying to impede the completion of my task.

"I promise you, Dunlock will pay for everything he's done. I swear it, on my life and my badge. But I need you to put the gun down," he pleads.

I hear the words—but at that moment, they have no meaning. A plea to spare the life of a homicidal maniac? Cops sure are funny. They're allowed to hate and hunt, but only to a point. They always quit right before they reach the edge in the name of justice or whatever.

I'm seeing red. His rationale is blurred by the color. Is he trying to tell me I've reached redemption's breaking point? That cozy place where you get to choose who you really are and what you truly stand for?

Dunlock cuts in: "Mi memba yuh… di likkle gyal who hold di gun just like yir doin naw. You're di one dat end yuh Fadda's life… nuh mi"

His judgment is a vicious slap on my cheek. He'd rather be dead than caged and he's baiting me to off him. In his arrogance, he knows his death will be another means by which he could elude justice and further control things by going out in his way—the warlord hero of his own story.

"Hey, you shut your mouth God Damn it!" Arturo barks. He turns to me, imploring: "Jeadda, please, you have a chance to do things right. I'm begging you to please trust me."

And then—just like that, my world slips back into focus. The reason I get attitudes toward the adulterous men at the club—The reason my heart weeps for the families of those whose lives I've taken—The reason my soul just may be redeemable.

Dunlock's face twists when I give up my weapon to the detective. Arturo cuffs him, making sure the shackles fit extra snug. I approach the man glaring into his eyes so I can reaffirm my choice by seeing what, exactly, is in there. What makes a man like him possible?

I see Nothing—and maybe that's my answer.

"I can't believe I let you control so much of my life. You're not scary at all. I want you to remember my face as the _**woman**_ who put you away for life," I say.

He smiles that ugly Pappa-Sangria Devil-man smile and I punch him square in his mouth. He spits out blood and teeth. Then he finally gives me the look I want: That of a man who has been defeated. It is deeply satisfying—'My Lord... yes, indeed.'

Minutes later, the Sirens crowd into the office. "What the fuck?" Dalia yelps, quickly assessing the situation and drawing on Carone.

Arturo returns the gesture. "Freeze!"

"Dalia, stop! He's trying to help us," Deseree insists, to deaf ears.

"Bullshit, he dies... now!" Dalia declares.

"Dalia, let him go... he's one of the good guys," I command. Although Dalia doesn't lower her gun, she eases a bit—she owes me that, at least.

Just then, the wail of approaching police sirens assaults our ears. "Hey, girls, we need to get out of here, like now." Jazmine cuts in, staring out the window at the oncoming lights.

"Get out of here. I'll take care of this," Arturo offers.

We grab Cofaxx and leave the room bundling into the elevator for the trip back down to our man-hole escape route.

CHAPTER 21

SISTERS

I learn later, that minutes after we escaped, several Scorpions storm the office. "Detective, are you okay, sir?" an officer named Sandusky inquires.

"Yeah, I'm fine. Here, take this piece of shit away," Arturo says. He turns Dunlock over to the officers.

Still, more reinforcements arrive, and the joint starts to resemble a policeman's convention as Gangsters are arrested—those that are still alive. Paramedics carry out the wounded and dead.

Sonny emerges from the mansion, carrying Candace's body. He lays her gently on a stretcher and kisses her one last time. Then he watches the ambulance take her away. Arturo places a consoling hand on his partner's shoulder. The two of them scowl at Dunlock as he and his bandaged nose are loaded into a squad car and taken away. Sonny makes sure to give him the finger.

Days later, the Sirens gather within binocular range of the cemetery where Candace's and my fathers were buried. Sonny and Arturo stand near her open grave as our grieving proxies. My dearest Candace is being buried, today. The detectives, somber in their actions, convene among her friends and family during her eulogy.

The preacher's speech is carried to us by the wind—that and the hidden radio receiver Madison placed in a tree shading the plot. "For as much as it hath pleased Almighty God in His great mercy to take unto Himself the soul of our dear sister, Candace Corin Smith here departed, we commit her body to the ground. Earth to earth, ashes to ashes, dust to dust..."

Cofaxx has his arm in a sling but he's healing. Dalia, still harsh and trying to fight being pulled back into the land of human emotion, wipes away tears before they can fall. Deseree, Jasmine, and Ryan embrace stand together in a sobbing circle. Shy Madison also cries, hiding in the SUV with the door open. We all feel it—the loss of a teammate—a friend—a sister.

Me—I don't have any tears left to cry, but my love for Candace will never fade or falter. I promise her that in my silent prayer. What can I say, this whole experience has given me a new perspective on all of the things I once buried inside my own, mental graveyard. I'm starting to believe that there is hope for me yet.

The ceremony ends and people begin to leave. "We'd better go too," Cofaxx suggests. We load into our vehicles and as we roll out, I take a final look at a nearby tree, where the initials of the Sirens have been carved along with the word, "Sisters."

Now—perhaps you're thinking, 'What a messed up ending to my story.' Well guess what, Smartass, I didn't say it had ended--

Approximately one week later, I stand in front of a full-walled studio mirror—not my bedroom but in an actual studio. The music plays and I absorb its beat launching into an emotional dance routine of my creation, set to a sweeping melody. It is **_my_** audition, after all.

Five judges sit at a table, eyes fixed, ready to determine my future. They have no idea who I am or what it took for me to be here. While I dance, I am bombarded by memories of more scars that may never heal, even as time mends my visible wounds. I think of Candace and I, laughing like silly kids; Cofaxx and I making love; Monica; Dunlock; my Pappa. They all spill out of me and I tell their story with my movements.

The music dissolves into another bridge—this one is a bass-enthralled, hip-hop track of my choosing. I included it as a triumphant piece dedicated to the new me.

I break into the latest hip-hop moves, revealing a fighter that was forged from loss. I am transformed into a Phoenix that soars out of the ashes. The judges sway to the beat, eyes wide, much like my sex-hungry strip club Johns. BAM! I complete my routine, knowing only that I left it all out there on the floor.

And that Pappa would be proud.

I grab my things and run out of the room, passing the long line of dancers waiting to audition, still unsure of my place—not even totally secure about the new me. I don't fully know her yet but I'm ready to learn more about her, court her even.

"Wait!" The call stops me mid escape and I turn cautiously. One of the judges has stepped out of the room. He beams at me and runs to catch up. For a moment, I almost expect a fight.

"Ms. Tibbaduax, you ran out before we could say anything." He pauses to catch his breath.

"Err... I'm sorry."

"I just wanted to let you know, that your audition was the best I've seen in a long time. You let your emotions guide you." His comment makes me wish Cofaxx was present to hear him say it. "We'd like you to join our Dance Company," he concludes.

"Oh my God, yes! Thank you so much!" I gush. Inside me, my heart begins dancing to my routine.

"We start rehearsal next Tuesday. Here's my card. Check the website for time and directions. And Jeadda... good job."

I take his card and study it to make sure it's real while he saunters back down the hall.

I quickly scoot out of the building before I accidentally combust and blow the place up with my joy. Once in my car, however, the waterworks start, and I scream with all of the force one might expect an ordeal like my life to demand. With nothing left in the form of fear doubt or shame, my cries are finally joyous and I thank God for his unmatched mercy. Though the storm was long and painful, I emerged victorious.

When my tears ebb, I turn the music up loud and drive off singing along with Beyonce's ***I'mma Diva***—Pretty fitting theme song don't you think?

As for my new sisters. We may not receive the praises routinely showered on public servants, but that doesn't matter much to us. The only reason I'm letting you all in on this Barbara Walters exclusive is so I can set the record straight, once and for all. Now that you know the truth, pass it on. We are not vigilantes murdering innocent people for a sick rush. We aren't crazed Fe-noms with extreme penis envy. Nor are we a bunch of bipolar Lesbi-ninjas.

We are just a group of ladies who saw the carnage being dealt out all around us and chose not to turn a blind eye to it. Because at the end of the day, Ignorance is Not Bliss and there isn't much relief for that naked twinge of fear that comes from seeing the chaos right outside your door.

Luckily for you, the Criminals aren't the only ones out there and the Sirens won't sleep until the streets are once again safe for decent people—that's a Promise. And I guess that's pretty much it.

For those Brainiacs and Anal-ists out there who want to know what the point of all this is—the moral to my story or whatever you call it. Well, if there is a message, I guess it would have to be that, no matter where you are in your life right now, it's not the final word on you. Let my story be an example that life isn't just what it is. 'LIFE IS WHAT YOU MAKE IT!

The simple fact that you wake up every day is proof positive that your story is still being written and you have access to the pen if you only dare to grab it. God's plan for you is still in the works, so I encourage all who read this to start living every day of this life like the opportunity for improvement, enlightenment, positive growth, and greatness it is. Never stop writing your story.

THE END—or is it?